FLUSHBOY

FLUSHBOY

stephen graham jones

DZANC
BOOKS

DZANC
BOOKS

1334 Woodbourne Street
Westland, MI 48186
www.dzancbooks.org

FLUSHBOY

Book design by Steven Seighman.

Published 2013 by Dzanc Books

ISBN: 978-1-938604-17-1
First edition: November 2013

This project is supported in part by awards from the National Endowment for the Arts and Michigan Council for Arts and Cultural Affairs.

Printed in the United States of America

10   9   8   7   6   5   4   3   2   1

for Skylar

and for Izzy

So there's video footage of me not washing my hands in the bathroom at work. My dad says it's the kind of thing that can tank his whole business. That he has to be extra careful. Don't I understand?

Usually I just stand there when he's spewing all this.

Last week I was his show-and-tell for Sunday school class. We wore matching ties, and I was under strict orders not to smile or look sly. Some of those people were his customers, after all.

I don't know.

Anyway, bam, yeah, the camera caught me: I ran the water but didn't wash my hands. Even pulled down a paper towel or two because that's the kind of thing you can hear through a metal door.

So, really, it's two crimes: bad hygiene and wasting paper towels.

My dad's real concern, though—this in front of the Sunday schoolers, his voice all reluctant—is the dishonesty of this act I've been committing for four months now, since he blackmailed me into working for him.

His concern is that if the city gives us a poor health inspection like everybody's waiting for, then his stupid little business won't catch on, go nationwide. In his eyes are dump trucks of franchise money.

Just two more years, though. I say this to myself a lot. Two years and then I'm gone, out of the wash high school already is, off to another state where I can enroll in some land-grant school and not tell anybody that I'm paying higher tuition. Not tell anybody what I did for an hourly wage my junior and senior years. I can be far enough away to forget the warm, anonymous Gatorade bottles I keep finding in the top shelf of my locker at school.

So, while my dad's lecturing on morals and business models and accountability, how to be a functioning citizen, I stand there moving my feet in my shoes, my lips careless, my hair half in my eyes. Of all the things I don't say, the main one is that we're a nine-hundred-foot establishment, remodeled out of the remains of a failed hamburger stand that was itself built on the ruins of an ancient gas station. What this means is that there was only ever one bathroom, a single toilet to serve both the sit-down crowd and the standers.

My question for him, if I ever opened my mouth during one of his lectures, would be, What are cameras *doing* in there, Dad?

Never mind that, if the health inspector ever finds out about this, it'll just be because my dad was sitting alone at a television set at three in the morning, his finger on a button that could have erased everything, just like it never happened.

Except that wouldn't have been right, I know.

But neither is this stupid job.

He's been standing
there like a zombie
all day.
　　　　—Mad Max

PART ONE

The Urinal Cake Blues

1.

I come on at four, right after school, and tie my apron and lower my hairnet and get my goggles in place before rolling the gloves on. By the end of the night the pads of my fingers will be pruned from sweat, and the skin around my eyes will be clammy from the goggles—my dad says safety goggles would do the trick, but I prefer the seal of the swimming kind, thanks—and I'll have earned between thirty and forty dollars of what, technically, should be gratuity. I know better, though.

It's shame.

I probably wouldn't care about my fifty-one other cents either. If it was even policy that employees could roll through the drive-through like a normal person.

We're not supposed to handle family either, but that's not so much an issue: I don't have any brothers or sisters, and, my mom, I don't know what I'd ever do if she ever came through. Probably kill myself. Will an aneurysm. Choke on my fist.

The girl who works the day shift, Tandy, she has five older brothers.

For the first few weeks we were open, when the news trucks were here every day to document the process, the phenomenon, her brothers were in line each lunch hour, just to razz her. Make her do her job.

Because it looks good on the six o'clock broadcast to have cars stacked in the drive-through, my dad looked the other way.

I assume that, anyway.

There has to be some reason he'd let policy slide for her and then jam me up for not washing my hands.

And before you ask, no, she's not the cheerleader/yoga type, Tandy. But then I'm not forty-four either, I suppose. Or a dad. On a black-and-white monitor, sitting primly on a toilet in a unisex bathroom, maybe she's every bit the cover girl. Or close enough.

Except—if the camera was actually aimed at the toilet, either head-on or from the top, then I'd have been busted for not washing my hands *and* for cigarettes. Unless my dad's letting them slide for some reason. And he doesn't let anything slide.

Five hours, I tell myself. Five hours then I can hand the keys to Roy, the night guy, the one who has to deal with the people weaving home from bars, who think our place is the logical halfway point to the drive-through wedding chapel they've always known was at the end of this road they're on.

The novelty's a big part of our draw, I know.

It doesn't make it any easier.

2.

Aside from it being the only shift my mom would allow me to work, the four-to-nine slot is what I would have picked anyway. Because the sun doesn't go down until seven-thirty or so. And daylight hours are the best, by far. Or, to say it differently, my dad's customer base mostly slinks out under cover of night.

While the sun's up, the drivers-through are just as embarrassed as you are.

Early on, my dad accused me of wearing my swimming goggles as a disguise, along with the hairnet, so nobody would recognize me. He was half-right. Because the job was supposed to be just temporary back then, I hadn't invested in any of the sleek Olympic models yet, like I have now, but was still wearing my old mask with the snorkel attachment molded to it. Like I was exploring some alien, underwater landscape. My dad calls it the "adult" world.

This from the guy who staged a fit when I declined his job offer, then moped around for four days and finally stepped into his bigger man boots, said he would just take that shift, then: be the proprietor, manager, *and* stand in the drive-through window.

This was fine with me, but then, sneaking in one night well after midnight—it was a Saturday—he was waiting for me in the darkness of the living room. I imagined him sitting in a wingback chair we'd never had. An evil chair.

I was under the influence of a couple of parking lot beers, sure, but that didn't change anything.

The voice he came at me with was the voice of the devil.

And it's not scary at all, that's the thing. It's simpering, kind of mewling. Like someone with hard shoes is standing on the knuckles of his fingers while he's talking, and he doesn't even want to be talking that much in the first place.

"Guess your mom laid down the law this afternoon," he said.

"I'm only two hours late," I cut back on instinct, my hand already on the banister, to pull me upstairs.

"What? No, I mean… an ultimatum. I guess that's what you'd call it."

I kept my hand on the banister.

"About the Hut?" I said, not because his tone was giving it away but because everything for the past year had been about the Hut.

In the thick air of the living room, my beer-tuned senses felt him nod yes, it was about the Hut.

"What?" I said, my eyes half-closed now, in a kind of innocent anticipation I shouldn't have even had in me anymore. In the later stages of my parents' ridiculous, days-long arguments, I mean, I usually ended up some kind of hinge point between them, able to tip things one way or the other. And I knew full well that the only way to avoid all that was to say nothing.

But this is why he was evil: he guilted me into that *what*.

"You know what an ultimatum is, right?" he led off.

"One of those organic tomatoes," I said. "Sure."

The flash of liquid white across the room was my father's smile. But then he covered it with his hand.

"She said if I—if I don't follow through on my promise, then, you know."

"No."

"It'd just be a trial thing. Nothing that serious."

"Dad."

"I shouldn't even be telling you this. You should just worry about your own things. How was school today?"

"It's Saturday."

By now my eyes had adjusted enough to see his velvety grey shape in the chair. He was holding one of his alcohol-free beers, the fourth one of the night, I'd guess, going by how weepy he was.

"You mean she wants you to follow through on your promise about how this one's going to work?" I said.

My dad hissed a laugh out through his teeth.

"It's going to work," he said. "That's not the issue. The issue is *who's* going to work."

"Dad—"

"Nobody's calling about the ad."

"Nobody?"

"Not the right person."

"I'm sure—"

"Listen, you just go on to bed now, cool? I've got some thinking to do. Whether I want this business to fail, too, whether I want to, you know, support my family, or whether I want to take that shift myself, then support my family from, like, I guess one of those Indian Village apartments, probably…"

The silence after this wasn't thick or cloying or any of that. It was stupid.

I understood now why he had the lights off: so he wouldn't have to see my eyes, accusing him, hating him.

"Somebody'll call about the ad," I said, finally.

"I'm sure they will," my dad said. "Until then, though—"

"I'll take it, okay? Just until you get a replacement."

The silence here was even stupider, because it was filled with my dad's pride. He was beaming.

He held his nothing-beer up, tilted it so the glass caught the moonlight, and asked if I wanted one.

It was supposed to be a father-son thing.

I went upstairs, dug through all my old boxes until I found my snorkeling kit, and didn't even notice for three weeks that the help wanted ad wasn't running anymore.

3.

I'm more religious now than I used to be. What comes around's been around before, all that.

When I was twelve and it was summer, all the kids on the block would have these running water gun and water balloon fights. Me and Greg Baines were the oldest two kids, so we got to soak all the third-graders to our heart's content, pretty much. And they liked it just because it meant we were playing with them.

I don't know.

Standing over them with Greg Baines once, this little kid's face and hair and shirt dripping wet, I felt a twinge of guilt that would eventually melt into shame, and make me stop hanging around with Greg Baines.

The thing was, all the water in our pump-up guns, it had been drawn from the toilet.

Now I'm that little third-grader.

My first customer dings the drive-through bell at twelve minutes after four, and the PA system outside cycles on automatically, instructing him to pull forward to the second bump, please, then turn his vehicle off, let us do the rest.

The driver catches my eye for a nervous instant—a Hut virgin, great—then eases forward, kills his car. Five seconds later the metal tracks grind on; they're from an old car wash from the sixties. My dad actually cried when he found them in working order. They're supposed to be able to deliver up to three tons of Cadillac or Buick or minivan or whatever from one end of our drive-through to the other, a total distance of maybe thirty feet.

So far, nobody's got stuck fifteen or twenty feet in.

If they did, though, it's not like we'd have to call the fire department. Just give them a golden rain check from the pad and apologize.

Anyway, every time the tracks grind on and the whole place shudders, my dad, even if he's across town, he smiles.

He really feels like he's providing the world a service here.

I want to touch a scratchy place on my cheek, but that would mean putting the rubber of the gloves to the skin of my face. Instead, I wave the guy in.

He approaches at what I've calculated is about six inches a second, all the junk on his dashboard dancing with the gears and chains under the tracks.

I stop his car when his window is even with mine.

"John or Jane?" I say, not because I can't tell but because it's policy to ask, just to avoid lawsuits.

"John, I guess," the guy says, no eye contact.

We could have this part automated, even have some kind of dispenser, forty-nine cents for a bottle or whatever—and my dad can see the day when that'll be the norm—but for now we're into the personal touch, into keeping things human.

Not to mention that it's hard for a machine to upgrade the sale. In my four months here, we've had nineteen sales meetings about "Selling *Up!*"

It works in the burger industry and it works at the lube shop, so why not here, right?

I've considered running away, yeah.

Many times.

"Privacy curtain, sir?" I say in my best cheerful voice, pretending that I actually am a machine, a dispensing unit. That the words have just been programmed into me; that his wheels on our moving carwalk—the track's painted yellow, even has one corner where my dad tried to stencil in bricks—that his wheels have activated my start button, my sales routine.

"A curtain?" the man stammers into his steering wheel.

I could be cruel here. If I make him wait, there's always the chance he'll wet himself.

Except I've made a customer service pledge, and am already on tape for not washing my hands.

I shape my mouth into a tolerant grin and show the guy the velcro at the top of the curtain, fix it to the fake headliner above me: a demonstration of what he can have for just an extra seventy-five cents. Nothing really, considering.

He nods and I pass it over.

"Gloves?" I say then.

They're in a tissue box like emergency rooms have. I hold them out the window.

"How much?"

"No charge, sir. We believe in hygiene."

He takes one, starts to take another, but I've already drawn the box inside the window again.

"Just one, sir, so we can keep this part of your experience with us free. If you want your own box for the car, however, for your next visit, you can—"

I don't get the eight-dollar box quite hoisted up into view before he's stammering.

"Left or right?"

"Either, both," I tell him, "whichever feels natural. And, in case of accidents—overspray's the industry term—you can have one of these windshield and dash wipes for twenty-five cents."

He takes two, is studying the leather interior of his car in a new way now.

The wipes were my mom's idea.

"What else do I need?" he says meekly.

He's exactly the consumer my father dreams about.

I hate it, but this probably *is* going to go nationwide. It probably *is* going to pay for my college.

God.

Next is the male lap-protector (*$.49*), which is just a round piece of hospital paper two feet across, with a hole in the middle—"for that extra layer of security"—and after that is the molded sponges my dad buys in bulk from the truck stop (*$4.00/each or 2 for $7.00!*), "for emergencies on the road or in the opera house," and after that, the guy's eyes already starting to yellow, an overflow canister "just in case" ($1.00 if used, $.25 if not), the packet of informational brochures, which includes our FM broadcast station numbers and a window decal, and then I've stepped off the button and he's easing forward, past the window, and I'm looking politely away, jangling the keys he wasn't aware he was going to have to leave with me, for collateral.

Not that drive-offs have been much of a problem yet—my dad says it's because of the "social contract"—but we'd probably be liable in some way if we were to give customers the opportunity to pee into a bottle with one hand and try to drive with the other.

I'm waiting when the carwalk delivers the guy up to the second window. It's been exactly fifty-two seconds: enough time to fill the bottle, shake off, and zip up.

Not that we're supposed to look anywhere but at the roof of their car.

He passes me the warm John and I mumble the total, push the stainless steel tray out. He fills it with whatever, I don't even look.

Aside from the smell of urine, the air of his car is thick with our FM broadcast. It's the sounds of burbling water. One of the early newspaper articles dubbed our station "KPEE"; it's part of our decal now.

I pull the money in, push his keys back out, and we're done.

All of us, I mean. People in general.

4.

In the downtime between customers, the suggested duties of drive-through personnel is to:

a) prepare more brochure packets
b) sort through the customer satisfaction cards and mark for action any that need action
c) restock the Upsale items

What I do is go back to the tanks and smoke a cigarette, one glove off, my goggles pushed up to my forehead.

There are probably cameras here as well, but screw it.

If I had my cell on me I could call Prudence, my girlfriend since sixth grade, but something about being so close to my dad's shop-made FM transmitter doesn't allow any signal to get through. Either that or there's so many news satellites trained on us that the bandwidth's all cluttered with attention.

Behind the tanks, like she's asking to be caught, are Tandy's cigarette butts. I usually sweep them up for her. Not because it's a safety hazard—I'm pretty sure that five hundred gallons of urine are only psychologically combustible—but because I could get blamed for them, have to do another Sunday school walk of shame or something.

When I see her, trading off shifts, we don't say anything, because there's nothing to say. We know where we are, we know what we do. On Saturday, the one day we each have off per week, should we ever be under the same food court or lobby or department store security camera, and somebody's watching us on that closed-circuit feed, we'll stand out, I know: the slumped shoulders, the slack face, the vacant, war-torn stare, like we've seen too much already. If ghosts could walk and mumble and wear clothes, that's what we'd be, I think. The only place we wouldn't stand out is the nursing home.

So, no, we don't need to be reminded about this by ever talking to each other.

As far as Tandy knows, too—as far as I know she knows—the new Spanish/English signs in the bathroom about mandatory hygiene procedures are just one more of the suggestions my dad's taken from his small businessman's handbook.

In case you can't read either Spanish or English, there's a diagram as well, a stick-person me, who, after he doesn't wash his hands, ends up outside the Hut, with X's for eyes and wavy lines coming off his hands.

Whether Roy can read or has to follow the diagram, I have no idea.

Unlike Tandy and me, he enjoys the job, always shows up ten minutes early, his thermoses of coffee slung all over his body, a non-regulation bandanna tied around his head, low over his eyes.

Maybe this is what third-shift people are like.

My father used to check on him, I know, ease through the drive-through in some elaborate disguise, trying to trip Roy up, but one night after a three AM spot-check I found my dad in the kitchen, slamming one of his fake beers so fast it was spilling down his chest.

When he looked at me, his eyes were blown wide, his lower lip trembling.

I didn't ask, don't think he would have told me anyway.

After my cigarette—I balance the butt on the emergency flush plug of the first tank, because I'll be back—I drape my right glove over my left shoulder and sort the day's haul of customer satisfaction cards. They're part of the packet of brochures we give. The customer can either drop them in the box bolted to the back of the building or they can mail them in.

Mixed in with the cards, like every time, are religious pamphlets and business cards.

At the bottom, though—at what would have been the top, before the box was emptied—are two tickets for the Bantams game tonight.

I look through my window, out at the city.

Chickenstein.

He was here.

Or she.

My hand shaking a little, I spread the rest of the cards and pamphlets across the counter, only stop digging through them when I get to the ones that are always there as well, the cards that are wavy now because they were wet before.

On one of them once, scrawled in pen, was: *sorry—didn't have anything else to write with.*

There's a reason we use yellow cardstock for the cards now, instead of the standard white.

I pull my glove back on.

5.

In my darkest hours, I allow the possibility of a convoy of out-of-state school buses nosing into our parking lot.

For vehicles too heavy for the tracks, policy is to walk the Johns and Janes out to the vehicle. This involves wearing the converted Whac-A-Mole tray that hangs on your shoulders with two padded hooks, like bass drummers in marching bands have.

In the slots the moles once lived in are overspray canisters and sponges and curtains and wipes and gloves and brochures. Twice I've found a coffee can, with change in it.

As the tray only carries eight used or empty bottles, what a busload would mean is about eight thousand sloshing trips, while trying to manage the drive-through as well.

Policy during an outbreak of service like this is to wear adequate back support.

I think my father is afraid I might sue him.

He thinks it's my back I'm worried about.

For the next twenty minutes, though, until four-thirty, no school buses appear on the horizon. Twice a blue Nova pulls up to the leading edge of the track, but each time she loses nerve, backs out.

The bathrooms a mile down at the truck stop are free, we know. "But not private." This is written in tempura paint on our front glass.

It's not all my father wanted the sign-people to paint, but there wasn't room for everything he wanted them to write, not if we still wanted the words to be readable from the street. So now we have brochures.

What they document is the inevitable development of establishments such as this one.

It starts a year ago at a Bantams game, where they serve beer. Where the urinals are in constant use, pretty much. The women's side as well. Aside from various hygienic issues (here my dad's supplied testimony from ex-custodial workers and pictures so close-up they look like scratch 'n sniffs), the opposing team—this is supposition, but it's hockey, too, and everything goes in hockey—somehow managed to replace the home side's urinal cakes with urinal cakes that had some of the properties of dry ice, apparently. The result was that for the second and third periods, the men's room was clogged with a sort of warm fog of pee: "the urine of a thousand or more gentlemen that night, mingling in your lungs." The result of *that* was an outbreak of bronchitis and sinus infections like the city had never seen. One old fan's death had even been attributed to the incident, though when Dad prints his name, he gives him his own special line, like a little headstone in the text. Like he's surrounding him with the moment of quiet he deserves. But he doesn't include an obituary picture, as we don't want to be sensationalistic.

The idea of breathing urine is enough, really.

What he doesn't say in the brochure is that some eight thousand male fans went home that night unaware, not coughing.

What he'd *never* say is that two of those fans were us.

To him it's not like lying. In business, he says, all is fair, so long as it's legal.

I don't think he learned this in Sunday school.

6.

Prudence shows up just before five, after her yearbook meeting. She sneaks around to my window, jack-in-boxes up to eye level and flashes her camera.

"Jane?" I say in my best customer-service voice.

"No," she says back, "Prudence, remember?"

It's our joke.

I let her in the back door. Somewhere in the city, my dad's having a heart attack.

"Any fish today?" she says, pulling the door shut behind her, touching the handle with only her fingertips.

I hook my head for her to follow me back to my station.

What she's talking about is how one morning Tandy found one of the Johns in the refrigerator, courtesy, we're pretty sure, of Roy. Swimming in the yellow-tinted water of the jug—light beer on an empty stomach—was a sluggish goldfish.

It had to be a joke, we're pretty sure. No fish could survive the urethra. Or, the truth of it is, we can't imagine the urethra that could be wide enough to pass a goldfish.

Because he didn't want to mess up our numbers, my dad cer-
emoniously poured the chilled urine and the goldfish into tank #2.

For all I know, that fish is still in there, invisible in the hearty
yellow water. Swimming through a dream it can't wake from.

Prudence, because she's like this, has named the goldfish Dick.

I like to watch her mouth when she says it.

Like I said, we've been together since grade school.

Twice a week, maybe, she'll close her eyes and let my hand slip
up under her shirt, but then she remembers something her mom
told her, I think, and she's batting me away, her hands soft, her
lipstick smeared.

So, yeah. If things shone in any kind of proportion to how
much you shine them, I'd be blinding people at the urinal.

She stays with me, though, and I stay with her, and lately she's
even started dropping the occasional aspirin in her coke, always
waiting to do it until I'm watching. At first I thought she had a
headache or something, but then she told me that when her mom
was in high school, all the boys were trying to slip aspirin into the
girls' cokes. The roofies of 1972, I guess.

They work.

On her aspirin and coke, Prudence can't hear her mom's voice
so well, and leans into me more, and laughs easier, more loopy, like
it's really getting to her this time. Like she might not remember
whatever inevitable thing's about to happen. Like it won't be her
fault.

It won't be long, I'm pretty sure.

Until then, instead of sex, we talk about fecal matter. Intimacy's
intimacy.

Fecal matter's the idea Prudence has been working on all week.
I'm supposed to pitch it to my dad.

She sits on the floor where the drive-through customers won't
be able to see her and repeats it for me, in the voice I'm supposed
to use to sell it: the obvious next step for a venture like this is a
covered patio diner out front, over the smooth concrete that used

to lead into the twin bays of the gas station, where the tanks are now. The tables are already there, even, from the six months the burger stand was alive. All we'd need to supply, really, is the food.

Not just any food, though.

Prudence's idea is that the only food people would buy at a place like ours would be novelty food.

And, in keeping with the theme, all the dishes would be made-up to look like turds of one kind or another ("Poo Burger," "S.O.S.," "Cowpie," "Rabbit Pellets," "Litterbox Cake," "Duty-Free French Fries," etc.), and the ice cubes would be yellow, and the pitchers would be Johns and Janes, and the waiters when they delivered the food would do it with their hands in bags turned inside out, and not look happy about it.

Then, going there, it would be a dare of sorts. Just to take one bite, even though it was just sausage or ground beef or whatever. Take one bite and hold it down.

I see her in Texas History 2, designing the menu in her red, decorated spiral.

"What about soup?" I ask her, eyeing a black pickup that's slowed to make sure this place is real.

"Tortilla," Prudence says. "With corn in it, right?"

I gag a little but try to hide it.

To her it's comedy, yeah.

I'm never pitching this to my dad.

"And we can have, like, carts, too," Prudence goes on, "like a roller coaster, that you can ride through the drive-through if you need to go."

"Just number one, though."

"Of course."

"I've got standards, I mean."

This is another joke. A complete joke. Over-the-top comedy gold.

While she's there two vehicles come through. One contains a husband and wife, obviously on vacation, who detoured fifty miles probably just to say they've done this—they buy every Upsale item I have to offer, and laugh and laugh, then give me one full bottle back (the Jane), along with one empty. The other car is a minivan driven by a desperate mother. She screeches into the emergency lane, the weight of her front tires starting up the red strobe lights.

Her four-year-old has to go.

I slide the John and Jane down the greased string, out to her open window.

In the emergency lane we don't slow you down by asking which you need, and because it's an emergency, you pay a flat fee for them both (*$5.00*), don't get any curtains or overflow canisters or kiddie models.

Instead of putting her keys in the bank tube that I'm pretty sure my father stole, the mother just throws them across the twenty feet.

They sail past my head in slow motion, ding against something behind me and bring it down with them.

"K-P-E-E!" Prudence yells from her place below the window, then melts into laughter.

I smile like nobody's said anything, and the tracks grind forward, the mother not at the wheel anymore at all, the minivan a ghost vehicle, abandoned.

Because I don't have a bank tube for her keys fifty-two frantic seconds later, I mime throwing them back. The mother nods, extends her hand, catches them exactly in the center of her palm.

What she mouths to me is *Thank you*.

The John she returns is slippery on the outside, and the kid's been eating crayons, I'd guess.

The red strobe light cycles down.

"Shit," Prudence says.

"Not on the kids' menu," I tell her, and she punches me soft then opens her hand on my side, nuzzles into my neck.

Like this, she has control, can stop whenever she needs to.

"Copro-lites," I whisper. "For the diet menu."

"It's *all* diet," she says back, right into my ear, "all you ever eat's one bite," and I eke a laugh out and give her the mother's two-dollar tip, tell her to buy a purple drink with it, to make her lips taste good.

"You trying to make me not hate you?" she says, standing up on her toes to stuff the bills into her pocket.

It's what we say instead of anything so stupid as *love*. That we don't hate each other.

"Kind of thought you already did," I say, rolling with the punch I know is coming.

Though policy is to wait until you have six, I take the three Johns and the one Jane to the tanks, and, just like I wanted, when I've got the wide cap of tank #2 backed off for the one Jane, Prudence balances up on the ladder and cups her mouth, calling in for Dick.

Her voice echoes, so that she's saying it over and over, and for the moment, anyway, I'm glad to be wearing the apron.

7.

Like he's psychic, my dad calls exactly thirty seconds after the door's shut behind Prudence.

"Yeah?" I say, trying to push enough boredom into my voice that he'll know it's just been business as usual.

"Checking in…" he says.

His voice has a definite false lilt to it.

"Consider me checked," I say, and pull down the door on the industrial dishwasher. Because there's not a full load of Johns and Janes, they have enough shoulder room to rattle up off the rack, careen all over the inside of the dishwasher. The steam fogs my goggles.

"So how's it going?"

"One hour down, y'know."

"No no *no*," my dad says, in a way that I can see him pacing with the phone, pulling neat little flip-turns at the end of his cord. "It's four to *go*. It's all about the attitude."

"Right," I say, the whole bay still steamed over. "Two hundred and forty minutes. Or do you want that broken down into seconds?"

Silence, of the restrained variety.

Which is fine with me.

The sales meetings he makes me and Tandy and a bleary-eyed Roy attend are always at seven on Saturday mornings, when nobody else is out. He calls the meetings classes, calls his school Drive-Through U. It's at the top of the clipboards we're supposed to take notes on. Until it became obvious he was the only one participating, he'd even try to lead us in a chant of sorts, one I could only repeat now under hypnosis.

The reason he holds the meetings on Saturday instead of Sunday, when there'd be even fewer people out, is that Saturday is the day *he* works the drive-through, because Saturday afternoon is where we are on the disposal truck's route, and he doesn't trust us to watch the drive-through *and* supervise the driver, make sure he's got all the fittings snugged down right. Either that or the rumors are true and he's fallen in with some porta-potty mafia or something.

According to an article in the financial section two months ago (it included a caricature of our "typical" customer), it's the only way a business like this can be making money. Because it should be costing more than forty-nine cents a pop to dispose of biologically hazardous material.

My dad's comeback is that the paper didn't factor in Upsales.

Really, too, I don't care.

What it means to me is a day off, instead of—and this is how it was the first two weeks—emptying each John and Jane into the toilet by hand, then flushing every fifth time.

As the city informed us, though, we were neither licensed for that volume of sewage nor was our plumbing rated for it.

So now disposal is off-site, and my father's sold his soul to some urine lord or piss merchant. One with goldfish swimming in his bladder, maybe.

"Listen," I say, before he can wind up into some lecture, "you know the Bantams are playing the Woodpeckers tonight, right?"

"Face-off's at nine," he says, his voice dropping a bit. "Got money on it, sport?"

"Just wondering if you could get Roy to come in early or something."

My dad breathes in sharp and then back out, as if it's painful, what he's about to have to explain to me. It'll have to do with overtime and employer/employee trust and frivolous stuff like hockey games.

Except they weren't always frivolous.

Without them, we wouldn't be where we are right now.

"Don't worry about it," I say, cutting him off again.

"I just don't understand how—"

"I said it's not important, Dad. It's probably too late to get tickets anyway."

This stops him, gives him something else to preach about: how I should plan ahead for things I want. Save and schedule and know what I want to do with my nights. And in addition, Roy's a grown man, who may have plans of his own.

"We'll talk about it Saturday morning," he finishes.

"I'm sure we will."

"Excuse me?"

"Nothing. Forget I said anything."

"Flush that frown?" he lilts, as if quoting.

It's a line from his chant. *Our* chant.

I hang up softly, look up into the fish-eye mirror, and realize what time it is: five o'clock. Shift change.

Lined up all the way to the street are cop cars.

8.

The story of Chickenstein is that he or she is worth ten thousand dollars. All you have to do is prove whether the person inside the suit is male or female.

Behind the closing credits of the news each night, there's some fool trying.

The most popular method is to break down the mechanics of Chickenstein's victory dance, show how this or that move is impossible for a guy or girl to do.

What this involves is stupid people wearing chicken-beak hats and dancing in their garage.

When I was a kid, I remember being so sure that every time I closed my eyes, the world changed, relaxed into its natural posture. That everything I saw was a big complicated play, being staged only for me.

Though I grew out of that, still, living in this town, it's easy to wonder if there's not an audience somewhere watching me, waiting for me to call bullshit on all this.

What's even worse is that the longer I stay here, the more I buy into it all.

Like the ice.

I'm not the one who called the radio station about it, but I was thinking it, that putting on your weekend sneakers and dancing in front of your mother-in-law's video camera is a whole different thing from strapping into the oversized feet of some chicken costume and dancing out there on the ice in front of thousands of people. You use whole muscle groups you probably didn't even know you had.

I'm not all sad that somebody beat me to that call, don't get me wrong. It just hurts to remember that I sat in the car for a couple of minutes after I got home, to be sure the caller got it right.

I don't know.

Half of the ten thousand is being put up by the Bantams, the other half by the parent company of the Channel 2 news and its sister radio company, and I don't know who's making money from the "Which came first?" shirts, which my mom thinks are a disgrace, an affront to public decency.

All of which is to say that, for Chickenstein, on game night, hitting the bathroom has become the most complicated trick in town.

Until my dad opened shop, that is.

Now, before each game and sometimes even during the second-period slump, when the cheerleaders are shooting t-shirts up to the crowd, Chickenstein will coast up to my window, in costume, and pay for a John and a Jane, take them both into the many folds of the Chickenstein costume, and then, before the second window, will have poured some from the John into the Jane, or the other way around, so that I can't tell anything.

And, though I'm sure it's trashing my dad's paranoid efforts to keep the urines properly segregated—why this would matter to the porta-potty overlords, I have no clue—what I do with those sacred half bottles is pour the first into the #1 tank, the men's, and the second into the women's, old #2.

The one time the next person in line realized what miraculous thing had just happened right there in front of him, the driver offered me eighty-three dollars for Chickenstein's "deposit." It was the driver's word, like we're a sperm bank or something. Eighty-three dollars was all he had in his wallet.

This was one of the days when my dad had us on alert, though. His health-inspector radar had been dinging all day.

It meant those eighty-three dollars could have been a test.

Not redistributing the urine is the first thing you learn at Drive-Through U. Not only would it contribute to the possible spread of disease, for which we could be held liable, but the service we offer is supposed to offer complete and total anonymity as well.

It's like you get brainwashed after a while.

So, no, I didn't sell Chickenstein's John or Jane that day.

But still.

Two days ago, sweeping the tracks, I found two fake chicken feathers. They were the color we all know.

And now those two tickets in the suggestions box.

That they were still there meant Chickenstein had come through towards the end of Tandy's shift. And, because it's still hours before the game, probably not in costume either.

The way that makes my heart beat is a betrayal of everything I believe in, yeah.

I do think it means I'm still alive, though.

9.

My father's term for the wall of police urine washing towards us at each shift change is "the bum rush." Because cops don't pay. It's not that they have a city tab we can charge, anything like that, it's that, the way they look at it, they're getting the coffee for free, right? It only makes sense that they should be able to dispose of it for free. And that it keeps them close to the radios, ready to respond, that just means we're doing our civil service. Helping keep the city safe. Doing our duty.

Their Johns and occasional Janes are dark and unhealthy.

You can tell a lot about a person from their pee.

Some smell like sugar, some like blood.

Policy is not to offer law enforcement any Upsale items. Because they'd take them.

For the next ten minutes, then, I process them through the drive-through like the cattle they are, and say *Yes, sir* a lot more than I mean it, until it becomes a sort of joke and one of the officers towards the end of the line asks what's so funny?

I lose my smile, hand him his John and then the overflow canister he snaps his meaty fingers for.

My face is hot.

There's no policy for this.

"You old enough for *this*, kid?" the cop asks, nodding down to his lap, pushing into the floorboard with his heels so he can get his shiny belt unsnapped. Holding my eyes the whole time.

I step off the button, let the track ease him forward, but not before he's already got his head leaned back in pleasure.

I'm glad Prudence is already gone.

On his radio something urgent is happening. The two black-and-whites still in line behind him light up, peel away, and the one already ahead of me at the second window just balances his John on the narrow ledge and squeals off the tracks, shaking everything.

Because these are cops and might need to blast off just like this, we don't ask for their keys.

By the time that last officer gets to the second window, his friend ahead of him has shuddered the tracks enough to splash pee everywhere.

Instead of giving me back the wet John, the officer, still holding my eyes as if daring me to stop him, pours its contents into a series of styrofoam cups he scrounges from his dash and floorboard.

"Sir—" I try to say, but I'm a gnat to him.

The same way you can't bring your own cups through the fast-food drive-through for refills—their policy is only to put their own cups under their fountains—we can't process any urine not in a John or a Jane.

That doesn't stop him from lining them like shot glasses on my bar, then taking out his pistol, wiping it down with a wipe he snaps his fingers for.

Pooled around his old coffee cups is more pee. The afternoon sky is reflected in its surface.

"Shouldn't you be flipping burgers?" he says, smiling.

"Don't you have a domestic dispute to settle?" I snap back just as bored, tilting my head out at all the places in the city that aren't this place.

This stops his gun-cleaning thing.

"Got a manager here, kid, or you all alone, like?"

I look away, lick my lips to keep my mouth shut, and hand him a pack of brochures, tell him to have a nice day.

He waggles the slick John up by his head, leans into his sunglasses and eases away.

With a pencil I promise to throw away so nobody'll ever put it in their mouth again, I push each of the styrofoam cups back out into the world.

10.

Instead of dropping the warm Gatorade bottles I find on the top shelf of my locker in the trash on the way to class, I set them behind me, just anywhere, and don't look around, even though I know there's some group watching me, waiting.

I've been written up four times now for littering in the halls.

On the fifth, I'll have to have a parent come up to get me back into school.

How I hold the Gatorade bottles is with a piece of torn-out notebook paper. It isn't a rubber glove. One of these days, the bottle's going to slip through the paper, crash into the ground, splash some jock's pee all over my legs.

At that point the joke will be complete, I think.

That isn't what makes me close my eyes each time I spin my lock, though.

What makes me close my eyes is that, since we got lockable lockers in the seventh grade, I've only ever had one combination: Prudence's birthday.

Whether she knows about the bottles or not, I don't know, and there's no easy way to ask. Especially not if I happen to be holding her hand at the time, or have designs on where my hand might be going later.

The nightmare in line right behind the one about the school bus of kids is the one where, twenty years later, my own children are looking at one of my old high school yearbooks and come upon a shot the yearbook editor has worked in near the fold and cropped down all skinny, as if she wanted to hide it, will be my locker, open, the Gatorade bottles clustered on the top shelf, the joke lost in black-and-white, so that I have to swallow it, say to my kids that I don't know what that's about, no.

The question will be whether the mother of those children—my wife—whether when it's her birthday, that combination of numbers will roll into place in my head, and I'll be holding my breath again, waiting, praying.

But I'd forgive her of anything, I think.

It's five-thirty. So many minutes to go.

11.

The brochures. If my dad spot-checks me and I don't have at least twenty packets rubber-banded and ready to go—his wet dream is some citywide sewage catastrophe, I think, forcing people to us in droves—then brochures will become the focus of the next Drive-Through U. intensive, and, midway through the demonstration, either my head will implode or the rest of me will become violent. Neither of which I want to have to deal with on my day off.

So, to save my Saturday and maybe my life, I slouch to the rack at the second window and fan all the slick pamphlets and brochures and decals out, start leafing them together in the recommended and, supposedly, market-tested sequence.

As for who that particular market was, I'm guessing it was my mother, reluctant and out of excuses at the kitchen table, my father sitting across from her, his fingers churched together, the toes of his loafers fluttering on the fake wood floor, the telepathy he's trying to direct across the table at her so thick you can practically see it.

We're on the ground floor of something big here.

This is the future.

That yellow glow in the pot at the end of the rainbow, it isn't gold.

These are all things we've found carefully printed onto the dry-erase board on the refrigerator.

Another: *Diuretics?*

They're what make people pee more.

But how to get them into every condiment tray and salt shaker in town? Or, better yet, how to condition the consumer so that, when he sees our distinctive sign, he has a sudden and wholly undeniable urge to relieve himself?

For the first month we were open, the rubber band that held the packet of brochures together was a delicate, made-to-break elastic string. It connected to the flare of each nostril of a series of Halloween noses we'd spray-painted gold. The noses were in honor of the sixteenth-century astronomer Tycho Brahe, our "proprietor in *spirit*." His family crest, altered just enough, is monogrammed onto the collars of our uniform shirts and painted onto the tinted glass of the front door.

He died in 1601 from a burst bladder, because it would have been rude to leave the party he was throwing.

According to the brochures, he's a lesson for us all.

As for the noses, Brahe had a prosthetic one, so my dad thought all his customers should as well, to properly display their corporate allegiance.

A plastic, golden nose, however, it's significantly different than a brand name artfully worked into the pocket of a pair of jeans.

There must be nothing about this in my father's small businessman's handbook. His *dream*book, my mother calls it.

Satan's bible, more like.

We still have boxes and boxes of the noses, and are supposed to distribute them with a "fraternal smile" upon request. It's a smile I've seen Roy attempt in a workshop once. He looked like he'd just swallowed a live lizard, and was trying hard to keep it down.

As for the rest of the brochures, there's:

- that legendary Bantams game and the rash of lung ailments that followed, all delivered in a very solemn, facts-only tone, and never allowing the possibility that most of the coughing people were trying to get in on a class-action suit, or that it was respiratory season already;
- the brief, pictorial history of urinals—a tour nobody wants to take, really;
- the historical uses of urine: tanning hides, flushing out wounds, making paint, hydrating the dehydrated, filtering mustard gas in some world war or another, marking territory, carrying disease, "paving dreams," etc., and not including "deviant" sex acts (my father's word);
- the support-group pamphlets: something from a Shy Kidneys Services, a "Paruresis—Do You Have It?" foldout from the American Urological Association, a "Nocturnal Enuresis" wordfind/sleep-aid, and, for *some* reason, an insert about how Porta-John Enterprises can supply facilities for whatever event you're having, be it black tie or blue-collar;
- and, finally, the thinly veiled, happy version of my dad's life as a small businessman, exaggerated in all the necessary places.

It's that last brochure I find myself studying sometimes, between customers. In it, my dad is idealized, perfect, predestined. Driven.

The other way of saying that is that he's got certain fetishes.

As a graduate student in biochemistry—this was before he defected to the land of business administration—his thesis (still "in process") was an analysis of amphetamine levels in the urine of truckers. The way he collected his samples was by taking assistants and volunteers with him into the unmapped wilds of the interstate ditches, to fish unburst plastic bottles up from the tall grass, a prize each time. The way he tells it, I can see him holding the trucker pee up to the sun, angling it back and forth so the light can glisten through it, bathe his face golden.

Due to a lack of volunteers, however—just one was hardy enough for the whole six weeks—the study had to be shut down, all the samples destroyed, and even then, my dad and his last assistant were there at the incinerator, taking notes about the color and tint of the flames.

To him it was a funeral pyre. The end of one dream, the beginning of ten thousand more.

After that there's a convenient fast-forward in the brochures, until the months leading up to that Bantams game that began all this.

For me, those were the last good times.

My dad's business then was a website—the first incarnation of The Bladder Hut, the way he tells it. What he doesn't say is that the main difference between the two was that the website was *consciously* entertainment-related. Instead of the forty-nine-cent freak show we have going on now.

Not that there wasn't a geek even back then, though.

There's always a geek, I think. Some kind of blockhead for the people to gawk at. At least where my dad's businesses are concerned.

His website was pnow.com. The only imperative URL out there, maybe. To his credit, it was a hard domain name to forget.

As to what he provided, it was a log of all the movies he subjected himself to daily, for full price, since the managers had locked arms, were refusing to work out any kind of deal with him.

What he was doing was posting the down times in the movie where an audience member could safely slip out to the restroom and not miss anything important.

The money wasn't meant to come from ad revenue, either; that was what he put down on his small business loan as the genius of his plan. His revenue was supposed to come from the programmed stopwatches he was going to sell that would glow or vibrate thirty-two or forty-one or however many minutes into your selected feature, usually about the time two characters started leaning into each other to kiss.

He wasn't writing reviews, but my dad's running critique came down to there being too much sex on the big screen. That nothing important to the story ever happened in bed.

Which is to say he was appealing to the sensibilities of an age bracket that no longer had the hand-eye coordination to manage one of his newfangled "pee-timers." Either that or people were still just hitting the head whenever they had to, like everybody except Tycho Brahe had been doing for thousands of years already.

But still, if I hold my eyes just right, I can see through this premature story-of-my-success stroke job and make out my dad hunched over his legal pad at the kitchen table, writing it all down the way it *should* have been. And after a while, it stops being hype, turns into a confession of sorts. A plea for help, which is at least the glimmer of an acknowledgment that something's wrong, right?

From there, then, it's just a nudge over to an apology, even the kind where you're looking away, covering your mouth with your hand.

Which is all I really want from him.

Instead, though, he won't even call Roy in a half-hour early.

This time when the drive-through bell dings, I finish the cigarette I've retreated to before lowering my goggles, dragging myself back up front, my lungs grey with smoke.

At which point the one nightmare I'd forgotten all about leans forward to see if I'm really in here or not.

It's my mom.

Here they come,
those feelings again.
　　　—Men At Work

PART TWO

The Great American Splashdown

12.

Because we're a facility that serves the public, the rule is that we have to have a public restroom. In single-toilet cases like ours, there has to be a unisex sign, a lockable door, a sink with eventually hot water and soap, and a last-serviced sheet at eye level with room for employees to initial.

Never mind that access to a public restroom takes money from our register.

My dad's solution is to arrange an obstacle course of OUT-OF-SERVICE and PISO-MOJADO signs and cones and tape all along the narrow hall, so that it's just bad luck that whatever wily customer's made it back this far chose *now* to try to use our restroom, instead of later, when it would surely have been available, or earlier, when nobody was even using it.

Just for appearances, though, we have to let every twentieth or thirtieth customer through. "At our discretion," of course, with eye contact all around, meaning it had better not be our friends' names that keep showing up in the guestbook, understand?

And if the freeloading customer's name happens to be *I.P. Freely* or *Ivana Tinkle* or *P. Rivers* or *Peter Pantz* or any fake-o

Indian name with 'Yellow Snow' in it, then it's our asses.

My mother's name is Gwendolyn.

It's not what she writes in the book.

Because she hasn't said anything yet, I don't know what to do.

"It's not really...out of order," I tell her, about the restroom.

She shakes her head no, not that, and looks out to the drive-through. A tumbleweed could blow across it at any time. "Has your father called?" she asks, watching me too close.

"A bit ago, yeah."

"And?"

"And nothing. Just being his stupid self."

This makes her laugh. It's not a good laugh.

Partway through it, a tear slips down her face.

I push the BACK IN FIVE / POTTY BREAK sign up against the first drive-through window. It's handwritten instead of printed on my dad's printer. I think Tandy made it, in a moment of desperation. Another emergency call to the suicide hotline number. Existential crises at The Bladder Hut.

I've found the sign hidden in every place here.

The name my mom wrote in the guestbook was *PP Dancer*.

It was what we almost called ourselves, *PP Dancer's*. The only problem was that it didn't end with a lowercase T, like 'Bladder Hut' does. And my dad needed that 't,' for branding purposes. The way it curves to the right at the bottom, he's turned it into a p-trap—that short-on-one side U of pipes under the sink. The rest of the letters are made up to look like plumbing fixtures as well.

Over the months leading up to the grand opening, there were so many other names, so many other designs, so many product tie-ins and pleas for corporate sponsorship, but none of that matters right now.

My mom is standing at the counter between the first and second window, trying not to cry.

For my sake, it feels like.

"What?" I ask.

"Your father," she says. "He's—his, you know. His beer. I don't know what to do."

"He's drinking again?"

She nods, bites the insides of her cheeks in an effort to control her face.

I study the wall, processing.

"*His* beer, you mean?" I finally say.

My mom nods again, quick, just once.

"The fake stuff," I add, trying not to sound too disappointed here.

Yes.

I blink her away for a moment, to collect myself.

Some days it's almost too much, being the only grownup in the family.

"Five before *dinner*," she whispers. A controlled shriek, really. A secret so vile she can't give voice to it all at once. I'm sure it's loud in her head, anyway.

What I'm thinking about is taking the potty-break sign down, just because any distraction now would be a good distraction.

Mellow Yellow.

The Golden State.

Drive-Thru John's.

Number One.

The Pit Stop.

The Whizz.

My dad had no idea what to call this place—*Urine Your Car? Nature's Call? Tee-Tee a Go-Go?* For a while there was even a fire hydrant involved. At the last moment, we were almost The P Spot, even. It was a compromise between The Bladder Hut and his P-Trap idea, and it even ended in a 't,' which has that curve going at the bottom.

It was serendipity, fate, providence.

In celebration, my dad had had an extra fake beer then, too, and toasted himself while we all watched.

There's a difference between toasting yourself and *getting* toasted, though.

His beer is like flat lemonade in a metal can that some kid's balanced up on the fence then forgotten all week. Even the cats won't drink it.

I'd think better of him if he'd just go back to the real thing, probably. Without alcohol to cloud his mind, the wheels in there turn too fast, grind us all up.

"It's okay," I say to my mom, peering up at her instead of hugging her, like I think a good son would.

"You don't understand," she says. "It's getting worse."

"He's under a lot of pressure."

"Since that hockey game, I mean."

"This is his dream, Mom. It *started* with that game."

"You're defending him now?"

She holds her hand over her mouth, as if just realizing she's going to be all alone now, so I hug her. I close my eyes where she can't see.

Two years, I'm saying to myself.

And that somewhere in her purse is a key my dad trusts her with.

It opens the case he keeps his security tapes in.

I'm not a good son. Maybe not even a good person.

That wasn't one of the job requirements.

All I need to be able to do this job is steady hands.

That cop was right, though. I should be flipping burgers, or drying cars, or mowing lawns.

My mom pats me on the back—we're both survivors, here—and then the walls around us tremble.

A car's in the drive-through.

Because I forgot to put the phonebook on the pedal that stops the tracks, they've already started, are grinding this confused customer past the first window, up to the second.

My mom pushes me away, smiles, and holds me by the shoulders.

"He's got you working until nine again?"

I nod, antsy to make that second window before the customer pulls away. For all I know, it's my dad.

Or Chickenstein, stopping off here before the pre-game festivities.

My heart slaps the backside of my chest.

"You should call Roy," my mom says then like a secret, just out nowhere, and my face goes warm the way it does when your mother's just read your mind.

The thing is, you wonder what else she might have seen in there.

"You know Roy?" I say.

"Just don't ask him about the—" she starts, but then seems to remember who she's talking to, and steps aside for me, makes her way back to the PISO MOJADO unisex bathroom she said she didn't need.

The thing is, KPEE's on a loop in here, and the walls are pale yellow. You always have to pee.

"Don't turn the lights on," I call after her, lowering my goggles.

She looks back to me for a flash but doesn't ask.

Or maybe she knows about the cameras.

While I'm waiting for the car to circle the Hut, come back to the first window, I hear the water in the bathroom splashing down into the sink.

The sign by the mirror says that hygiene's easy.

Not that my mom can see it in the dark.

13.

Five minutes after my mom leaves for her book club, I'm still standing at the first window, waiting for that customer to get his or her nerve together, wrap back around.

It never happens.

Instead, what angles into our cracked parking lot is a long shiny bullet of a limousine, its windows slick black.

Our policy for this is to treat this person just like any other and not ask the chauffeur what the limo's tipping the scales at.

Even if the tracks do seize up under the weight, it's advertising, right? A media event in the making, as soon as whoever it is opens that back door, lets his or her leg descend to the diamond steel plate, eyes unreadable behind perfect sunglasses. It'll practically be an endorsement.

I want to scratch my cheek again and do before I remember that I'm wearing my gloves, and then become sure that the germs are inflaming my skin, giving me instant red welts, making me look like a freak for this celebrity.

Even janitors don't have to wear swimming goggles to keep the hepatitis out of their eyes.

I lick my lips, another thing I've promised not to ever do in here.

The chauffeur eases up, tilts his head back to see me better.

He's the bodyguard/driver model, I'm pretty sure.

"The works," he says, both hands on the wheel, his words clipped and proper.

From the cavernous spaces behind him, a girl laughs, tries to muffle it.

The corners of the chauffeur's mouth don't so much as twitch.

"How many?" I ask, nodding to the idea of his passengers.

The chauffeur considers this, nods to himself, and passes me a crisp fifty-dollar bill.

"Will that cover it?" he says.

I nod yes. My hand is shaking. I hope he can't tell, but of course he can.

"Your…the ignition keys," I manage to get out.

He narrows his eyes about this the slightest bit, cocks his head as if for confirmation but then nods to himself, pulls the single key from the ignition, holds it up for me.

The limo doesn't miss a beat, just keeps idling.

There's no policy for this.

I take the key, put it in the plastic bowl.

"Don't bother with the escalator," he instructs me, dropping the limo back into gear. "They've got drinks back there."

I nod, swallow.

The chauffeur smiles, his eyes kind, and hands me another ten. It's folded longwise. This is code somehow that it's just for me. I don't know how I know this, but I do.

"Can I ask you a personal question?" he says then, as I'm palming the ten out of sight.

I look up to him, and down along his long, spotless car.

"If you happen to cry in those," he says—my goggles—"do they fill with tears, and what does the world look like then, and can a person drown in this manner?"

I grin like it's a joke and keep my weight on the pedal, and pass John after Jane after John to the slender, naked arm that reaches up from the parted rear window of the limo.

It takes them a full twelve minutes to make it the fifteen feet to the second window, and the amount they live during those twelve minutes, it's more than I've lived in my whole sixteen years.

14.

Though The Bladder Hut was christened on the news four months ago, with a beer bottle instead of champagne, part of Tandy's assigned morning duties is to spray down all the outside walls with the pressure hose.

People are still christening us is the thing.

The idea, I think, is that if it's a little bit of a rush to pull through the drive-through that first time, hand somebody a tall cup of your hot piss, then, dude, imagine the rush of sneaking up when Roy's not looking, letting loose a stream against the wall and *not* paying for it. Running away and trying to zip up at the same time. Tripping over yourself. Laughing.

Now the stucco from about thigh-level down all around the Hut is a slightly different color than the rest. Like from sprinklers, except there's no grass for blocks in either direction.

As far as the city's concerned, these nocturnal emissions—that's my dad's euphemism—are our fault. We've made ourselves a target, are asking for it.

My dad isn't surprised by the city's stance here.

It's human nature to resist innovation, to want what's behind instead of what's ahead. To the Indians and pioneers—this is in the brochures—the idea of a "bathroom," of doing *that* in one place day after day, it was pure comedy, a sure sign that this new-fangled civilization was only temporary.

He only works the drive-through once a week.

This allows him to see the whole thing from that kind of distance. As history.

He's never had to hold a John or Jane up to the fluorescent light, shake it to be sure those are ice cubes in there. He's never had to decide whether straining a floating bill from a bottle of pee is really worth it or not.

Once I even had a guy in a landboat of a Buick shriek in, two cop cars overshooting, getting locked up in the intersection.

It took them fifty-two seconds to park, get out of their cars, slam their drunk driver up against our rough wall.

By that time our transaction was complete: he'd poured all his bourbon into a forty-nine-cent John and paid me to take it.

It was a rich golden color, like the urine of a person with a kidney infection, and the vapor rising from it made my eyes water.

I was in training, but I knew the first rule by then, too: you don't redistribute. Even for the cops.

Civic duty, all that.

The only name I ever contributed to my dad for this place was Jerkwater Station, Inc., a subsidiary of Aimwell.

Because everybody was having a voice that night—these were the desperate hours—my dad had set his teeth, scratched Jerkwater onto the list.

My other idea was a discount card of sorts, for members. The Main Vein Club. You'd get a monogrammed John or Jane every twentieth visit.

This was all when I was never going to work here.

What I wrote on the dry-erase board in the kitchen this morning, in neat, blocky letters, was that, after latrine duty (*0400–0900*),

I was probably off to my Lizard Drainers Anonymous meeting, to "flush all my problems away," and that no, I'm not pissed off. Kind of the opposite of that, really.

I thought that was what my mom was here for.

Just thinking about her in the drive-through makes me need another cigarette.

I wind my way back to the tanks, squat down in the shade of five hundred gallons of urine and breathe in the only air in this place I trust.

On the slick concrete between me and the door is the over-spray from when we painted the Tycho Brahe noses gold. My dad or Tandy or somebody's tried to cover it with exactly twenty-two of our first run of promotional stickers, from before "KPEE" caught on.

Need to see a man about horse? they ask, in alternating colors. There's an actual cartoon horse smiling behind the question, too, with a racing number draped over him (*or do you just need to p!$$ like one?*).

It's complicated, the urine business.

I almost smile but catch myself, lean back instead to blow my smoke straight up, and that's when I see the impossible: four thick black fingers wrapped around the edge of the wide mouth of tank #2.

The lid has been eased back.

From the inside.

I fall back, try to run, but my shoestring is tangled in the plug of tank #1 somehow, the fingers up there slowly becoming a hand, the hand an arm, the elbow cocked up for leverage.

Because God loves me, my shoestring finally snaps and I shoot forward, and, because he loves me even more, my aim is off.

Instead of crashing through the door to the plastic orange safety cones of the hall, where the floor *isn't* wet, my forehead connects in a very solid way with the metal frame of the door itself, and the last thing I think is crystal clear: that I can't swim when I'm knocked out.

And then nothing.

15.

As far as my dad is concerned, I'm sure, the ten or fifteen minutes I'm unconscious is the worst kind of employee dishonesty. I'm stealing money from him. Lying down on the job.

He's not here, though.

And somebody's put a rolled towel under my head.

The place smells almost exactly like a rest stop restroom, the kind that only get serviced once a month, when the rains come in around the incomplete cinderblock walls.

For a moment I think that this is my punishment—or, no, a gift. That I'm getting to start over, that I've been deposited back in time, to that Bantams game where this all started, so I can part the yellow mists, reach down into the urinals, carry all that bad urinal cake out to the parking lot. Stop all this from happening.

What's really happened is that my shoestring dislodged the plug on tank #1, "Old Faithful" (my dad calls #2 "Annie," I don't know why—except that around my mom, Annie's just "#1"). Not all the way, but enough for a thin, focused rooster tail of pee to shoot up, all that pressure behind it.

I only find this out when I lift the towel draped over the plug, of course.

The line of pee is aimed right at my crotch, as if it too has a memory.

I swivel to the side, let the towel fall back down.

Up front, somebody's whistling.

I roll my fingers into a fist about three times. Not to fight my way out, but just to think. To try to make this make sense.

I've gone too far, though. Have been there for months already.

When you work at a drive-through urinal, you get to a point sooner or later where you're just accepting things on faith. And then repressing them just as fast.

Instead of rising, the pee I've let loose in the bay swirls towards a small rusted drain in the center of the floor.

Up front, the second window opens, slides back shut, and the register dings.

"Dad?" I call out, weakly.

No response.

The lid of tank #2 is shut again. My cigarette is fizzled out on the concrete.

I slush my way to it, guide it to the drain.

Destroy the evidence. It's an instinct.

And then a black form darkens the hall for an instant, in passing to the first window.

I fumble another cigarette to my mouth, light it, and sell my soul to the devil: if that can just be my dad, who cares why, then I'll let him see this cigarette. Even ask him to tell me all about the dangers of smoking. Hold my wrists out, together, and throw myself under the disapproving glare of his Sunday school class.

I smoke until my lungs are hot, my eyes red, then turn my head sideways as if walking into a wind and move down the hall, the fingertips of both hands always touching the walls.

Standing at the first window, in a full-body wetsuit, hood and all, is Roy.

"I thought you were Dick," I say, by way of hello.

"What you calling me?" he snaps back, winking at me the way he always does, which is the way your uncle who smells funny winks at you, the one your mother won't let you be in any room alone with.

"Goldfish," I say.

Am I going to faint?

Is this one of the dangers of smoking?

"They're like the rhinoceros," Roy informs me.

The question must be written on my face, because Roy answers: "Rhinoceri and goldfish live from moment to moment, have no real memory. The rhinoceros, however, *his* moments"—he laughs, in appreciation I think, or maybe jealousy—"they're as long as our days. It's a world of scent for them, and moments only become other moments when the wind comes through. Whereas the goldfish is swimming *along* a series of instants, I guess you could say, each as new as the last. Like *he's* the wind, you know?"

"You were in the tank," I tell him, because he's obviously forgotten.

He does his shoulders like he's caught, yeah. What now?

"Get that plug kicked back in?" he asks then, leaning back to see if a pair of early headlights are about to blind us. They don't.

I shake my head no, Roy, I didn't get that plug kicked back in.

He smiles and leans forward, does his fraternal smile thing that makes me shiver, and says, "Did I hear right, about Cybil Leon?"

I narrow my eyes at him, lean back just a little.

His black wetsuit is still glistening.

He holds up his earbud to show what he means. The wire trails down to some inner pouch in his suit.

"Cybil Leon," I repeat. "The singer."

"She's in town for the game," Roy explains.

I close my eyes, open them, try not to blink.

"You—you were *in* there," I say again.

He reaches under the counter, agrees with me by leaning a sil-ver diving tank out from under the counter. It's left a wet ring of pure corruption on the floor.

I open my mouth to say something, I'm not sure what—that he should have used a coaster?—but then say something else instead: "Those are my old goggles."

Roy looks up to them on his forehead then back to me.

"You were done with them, right?" he says.

I hold my lips together and nod.

Very done, yes.

16.

Instead of Tandy's *POTTY-BREAK* sign, Roy threads his own up from some crevice of the counter I never even knew existed. It says, simply, 'Gone Fishing.'

I touch my nose with the pads of two of my fingers, and regret it.

"Is that it?" Roy's saying from right beside me.

I follow the line his arm is making.

He's pointing to the plastic milk tray of Johns and Janes from the limo.

Cybil Leon.

"Maybe," I say.

Roy smiles his real smile. It doesn't make me any less uncomfortable.

In six eager steps, we're standing on either side of the tray.

"What do you want for it?" he says.

"I don't know which—"

"For all of them," Roy says, lowering himself to their level. Maybe to make out any telltale particulate matter.

The pee is bubbly and light, like champagne.

I cough, can't stop for a few breaths.

Roy pats me on the back. It doesn't help.

"You were in the tank," I say for the third time.

It's a question. I'm just having a hard time with the words of it.

Roy shrugs, looks at me kind of sideways, as if wondering if I'm for real here. If I can really be this stupid.

"You mean your dad never told you?" he says.

I shake my head no.

"In grad school, we traded off, man. We were buds. I'd help him with his project if he'd help me with mine."

"The truckers."

"Clowns of the highway is what they are."

"You were in school with my dad?"

"He's kept you locked in a closet, or what?"

"It's not in the brochure."

"Yeah, well. Let's just say those brochures, they're a little bit... incomplete?"

I nod, am not real sure what I'm agreeing to.

Roy pulls me into the hall, as if he knows that's the one place up here that's not bugged. And still he whispers.

"His thesis was small-time, man. Speed in trucker piss? Wonder if there might be, like, *salt* in the ocean too? 'Let's do a study.' Whatever, though. But I was there till the end. Don't let his sorry ass tell you any different."

"Six weeks."

"That was the first tour, yeah. The methodology was flawed from the get-go, though. I mean, nothing against your dad, but he didn't have a control group, we didn't know what trucks had come from where, or whether ultraviolet light was breaking the proteins down, of if the bottles were all-the-way empty in the first place, any of that. Your old man's idea was that if you just got enough urine, then the truth would somehow magically reveal itself."

"He's like that."

"No shit. I don't mean to talk bad about him. Being hopeful's a good thing. We should all be more like him probably. It's the rest of us who do the real work, though, right? I mean, his study got canned, man, bing-bang-boom. But they couldn't stop mine."

I look down the hall to the tanks, then track back to Roy. To my old snorkeling mask. You're supposed to spit in them to make them work underwater. I can't remember why.

"Since historical times, urine has been used as a curative, right? But that's just the surface. Have you ever heard of sensory dep tanks? That's for 'deprivation.' Like, you just float there in space, and nothing can touch you."

I have heard of these, yes.

Roy smiles like that's all I need here, then. He opens his hand to Old Faithful and Annie.

"Imagine, instead of water, using the body's own *fluids*, man. Did you know that urine rises to match your body heat faster than any other fluid? Like it *remembers*. Like that's where it's most comfortable. But that's not what I'm talking about."

Through the drive-through, somebody in a fast, low car is watching us.

I can't imagine what we look like.

"Think about it," Roy goes on, his breath harsh and acidic, because he's crazy, and has been immersed in a vat of pee for however long a scuba tank lasts. "That's all I'm saying. It's the perfect inversion, like. I mean, urine, it's usually in the bladder, in *us*, right? But this, going in, it turns all that inside out. Now *you're* in the bladder, man, and the urine's all around. And, people don't know this either, but the buoyancy properties of urine, we're designed to float precisely in the middle of it. Not bob up, not sink, just *be*."

The sports car in the drive-through has backed up now, is easing forward again, trying to start the track.

Roy's got the phonebook on the pedal, though.

"Listen," I tell him, looking down the hall to the tanks again, "there any chance you could clock in a half-hour early or so tonight?"

Roy rubs his nose more than is really necessary, especially with the gloves he's wearing.

"Maybe," he finally says, no eye contact anymore, like we're do-ing something criminal here.

It turns out we are.

"For Cybil," he whispers.

I flick my eyes in the direction of the milk tray from the limo.

"But that's the first rule," I whisper back.

"And I won't say anything about this either," he adds, pinching the cigarette from my lips.

I look to the drive-through and nod like I know better, and he's already at the second window somehow, hugging the lightest colored Jane to his black rubber chest.

"Eight-thirty," I call over to him. "Face-off's at nine."

"If I'm back by then," he says.

"Where are you going?"

"Pre-game," he says, winking at me again, so I feel it in the base of my jaw. "If she signs it, that's proof, hoss. *Proof!*"

I press my palm into my forehead, don't even care about that contact anymore.

"Eight-thirty," I call out again, then lower my goggles, belly up to the counter of the first window.

"Sorry," I say in my customer service voice, flipping Roy's sign away. "We were having some technical—"

"—difficulties, yeah. Kind of thought it must be something like that."

It's my dad.

17.

Because he's a small businessman, my dad doesn't put a sign up at all. He just follows me from window to window for the next twenty minutes.

"What if I had been the health inspector?" he says.

I'm not supposed to answer.

"What if I had been in the emergency lane? You know we're morally responsible for any accidents that happen out there due to our inefficiency, don't you?"

This is going to be in class Saturday morning, I know.

"PP *Dancer*?" he reads from the log.

I don't know if he's read the dry-erase board at home yet or not. Maybe I can still beat him there somehow. Because, after this, it's not going to be the perfect thing.

"Mom called," I lie. Just to slow the tirade.

It works.

"She was looking for you."

"What did she say?"

"She said, 'Where's your father?'"

"I didn't ask for any lip."

"I'm just answering."

He still hasn't been in the bay, doesn't know about the leaky plug.

Spread out on the counter in disgust are single-serve condoms. They're from the Planned Parenthood Coalition. Their idea is for us to package them with our brochures. My dad doesn't see the connection between The Bladder Hut and teenage mothers. I don't think I do either.

Agreeing with him now's not going to help things, though.

I give him the day's haul of business cards from the suggestion box, and it keeps him in one place at least, filing them.

"Did your mother say anything else?" he asks.

"Why?"

"It's her book club night."

This is not an answer.

Last year, even, it was our excuse to slip away to the Bantams on Tuesdays and Fridays: because she was over at her friends', talking about literature.

I don't know what my dad does with his evenings now.

Hits the fake bottle, I guess.

Spot-checks his employees.

Brainstorms.

"I know why you wouldn't call Roy," I finally say, during the fifty-two seconds I have between the first and second window. It's some business guy, who specifically asks for two overflow canisters and then starts in on an elaborate explanation just why he needed them.

Because my dad is sitting there, I listen patiently then ask how much it costs to have a tie dry-cleaned these days?

It's a polite, scripted conversation.

By the end of it, the businessman's wearing a reusable tie-clip shaped like our p-trap and has been relaxed enough to do his business confidently in the privacy of his own car.

I'm a product of Drive-Through U.

There should be a bumper sticker.

"Let's leave Roy out of this," my dad says, not looking up.

"You could have told me."

"That's not why I'm here."

"On Earth, you mean?" I say.

"Tonight," he corrects.

I narrow my eyes, concentrate on getting the businessman's dollar eighty-three into its proper places in the cash drawer (*one John, $.49; one overflow canister, used, $1.00; one overflow canister, unused, $.25*; the tie-clip is free, just on the chance that he'll forget it's there).

"It's about your mother and me," my dad says, filing a card he's already filed two times. I know because it's the wavy one with the pink edges.

I stop polishing the counter, angle my head over so I won't miss any of this.

"We want you know that it's not your fault," he says, and then a scared woman in a large van saves me.

"What do I—do I just—?" she says, her pupils blown wide with fear.

I lead her through it, don't even take advantage like I should, with the curtains and wipes and lap protectors. Not because she's delicate, but because I think I am.

In the end, because she's too nervous, I have to give her the glove.

My dad rises, my obedient, mute helper, and takes the glove from the refrigerator, puts in the microwave.

The glove turns and turns, the therapeutic gel inside it heating up and holding that heat in.

When the light goes off, I walk the glove to the woman, tell her about KPEE, and make a show of looking away, back to the bay.

The glove's supposed to trigger the same response as putting a sleeping person's hand in a bowl of warm water.

Recommended usage is to wear it on your off-hand. It's complimentary.

If the customers can't go, then that's the beginning of the end of The Bladder Hut.

My dad is waiting for her at the second window. He holds her Jane up like a newborn, like we should all be proud, then, in solemnly passing her the brochures, ceases to be a doctor, becomes more of a funeral director, I think.

When she's gone, we're left with just each other.

"That's why I'm doing this, though," I tell him. "So y'all won't have to...you know. You *said.*"

My dad wants one of his fake beers, I can tell. All of them, maybe.

"She stayed with me through the dark years," he finally says, not in his dad voice, but his narrating voice. Like he's dictating another brochure.

"The dark years?"

"Before the Hut." Now he's just reciting. "She never left me. Every time an invention or a business didn't pan out, she stayed with me."

"You don't think there's a reason for that?"

"Then..." He collects himself, starts over. "It's finally working, though. We're making money. I mean, people pee. Death, taxes, and us, right?"

I nod, a little bit afraid.

"Why *now*, then," my dad asks, "instead of all those other times, when she probably should have left? When I never even understood why she didn't?"

I'm not supposed to answer these questions.

That isn't to say there isn't an alarm going off in my head. I'm almost surprised he can't hear it. That I haven't started bleeding from the ear.

What I'm thinking, what I'm trying *not* to think, is that ever since my mom's book club started, I don't think I've ever seen her propped up on the couch, reading.

Where *is* she those nights, then?

18.

My dad skulks off, his warped business cards still spread out on the counter, not even alphabetized. He's not the proprietor he once was. I almost want to do something loud and wrong, just to get him all wound up again. Kickstart his small businessman instincts. Get him detailing some obscure point of policy until he's forgotten himself, is citing verse and chapter.

Instead I call Prudence on the Yellow Line. It's for emergencies only, and having my lips that close to holes Roy's probably ordered pizza through makes me want to gag.

"Hey," I say when she finally finds her cell. My hope is she'll be able to get from that one word a full report of what's going on here.

Instead she says my name back to me, like a question.

"Yeah," I say, switching ears, leaning down even closer to the antique receiver. "Where are you?"

Geographically, I mean. Because I can tell she's not alone.

At a few minutes after six, she's usually splitting some kind of salad with her mother. They're not vegetarians, quite, but they won't eat anything that ever had bones.

This doesn't include ice cream. Or, I'm hoping, glorified bathroom attendants.

"What?" she says.

"Where are you?"

"Did you know there's a game tonight?"

"It's Tuesday, yeah. That's what I was calling for—"

"Playing the *Wood*peckers," she interrupts, whoever she's with laughing about the name with her.

I don't think she's hearing everything I'm saying here.

"I might be getting off early," I say louder, like I'm insisting.

"What?"

"My mom is leaving my dad!" I yell.

This quiets her.

She says my name again, is trying to hush the voices around her.

"Serious?" she says.

"Serious," I say back.

"God."

"Exactly."

When she doesn't have anything else, I ask if her mom'll let her catch the game tonight.

"You're working."

She's in a wind tunnel, I think. Maybe having a hair-dryer fight.

"Roy's coming in a half-hour early. We can still make most of the first period."

"I didn't—you should have told me this earlier."

"What? I didn't know until—"

"Nothing. Listen, I don't know. My mom…"

She trails off, is a terrible liar.

I'm staring at the yellow wall now. At the pale yellow phone cord swirling towards it. Like I'm floating in space, peeing into a black hole.

"Hey, customer, I've got to go," I tell her.

"What about your mom?" Prudence asks back.

I cough, blink.

"What about yours?" I say back, quiet enough that she doesn't hear. "Eight-thirty, okay? Roy's coming in early. He promised."

Silence.

It makes me smile in pain.

"Love you," I sign off.

"You too," she says back, but that could be the answer to anything.

I hang up, go back to the first window.

It's dusk, every third car's headlights glowing on.

None of them are in my drive-through.

19.

For the studies that must have gone into the John and Jane, I don't think there was any control group.

If I was in charge there wouldn't have been anyway.

All I would have done is collect twenty or thirty people, even parts men and women. All weights, heights, ethnicities, orientations, affiliations, temperaments, whatever.

They'd all think they were coming in to fill out psych-profile bubbles or something. I'd even tell them not to worry about number two pencils, the lab has enough to go around.

But then, once they were all in one room, there'd be some kind of earthquake or avalanche or nuclear war or alien invasion or pathogen or pollen hurricane or something. Zombies, even. Some good reason for us to keep the doors locked.

And, because these surveys were only supposed to take an hour, ninety minutes tops, the room wouldn't be equipped with facilities. But—and this you circulate, instead of announce—we do have this one closet, a certain product still in trials, and then another closet, that has all kinds of elbow room, a lockable door, and one light bulb on a pull chain.

By this point in the testing, the Johns and Janes would have already branched off from the fantasy of a single, one-size-fits-all bottle. So there would be the male model and the female model—pink and blue, maybe.

That's not the genius of it, though.

The genius is that these experimental designs wouldn't be made out of the hard plastic they are now. Instead, the top few inches would have a consistency only slightly more resistant than wax.

This is to preserve the shape the individual mouths get pressed into, because the reservoir part of the Johns and Janes isn't the problem. All that's necessary with the reservoir is that it be somehow below the mouth of the thing, so that gravity can keep the urine from surging back up.

The mouth, that's the part that can't have any flaws.

It's like the docking apparatus space ships and space stations have: if the seal there isn't perfect, then there's going to be astronauts floating around where they shouldn't be floating around.

The reason I like to think that this was how the study worked is because—at least this is what I thought before talking on the phone to Prudence—people are basically good and not evil and ignorant and careless.

Growing up with the parents I've grown up with, I had to imagine that there was something better out there. Because if there's not, then the first time your mother leaves you alone in your room, you set a crayon into the corner of your left eye, get the balance right, then lock your fingers behind your head and slam your face into the wall.

More and more, though, I'm thinking maybe that *is* the world I live in. That there *was* actually a lab out there where people had to pee into a series of bottles, starting with the beer bottles everybody's tried at one time or another and then graduating to the roomy mouths of Gatorade bottles—wall-bangers, my dad calls them, like he's unaware what this says about him—and the bottomless reservoirs of milk jugs, then different kinds of beakers, novelty containers like come with popcorn at the movies, and on and on, always somebody standing right there over your shoulder taking notes. Asking you if it's uncomfortable to sit in a warm pool of your own piss. If it was the angle of the bottle or the shape of the mouth that caused this, or whether it could have been user error.

I don't know.

Where is she?

I'm talking about Prudence, but I guess this could go for my mom now too.

What I'm really saying about the Johns and Janes, it's that I hate my dad.

Somewhere in his cabinet of videotapes are the manic, round-the-clock training sessions we had to endure in the days before grand opening.

Part of it was to sit behind a curtain in the bay, on a bench seat looted from the junkyard.

This was to get us in the frame of mind of the customer.

In our hands, fresh from the refrigerator—this was when we were still keeping them there, then walking them to the toilet five at a time—either a John or a Jane.

Our instructions were simple: pee in the bottle.

My dad, of course, had been prepping us for this all morning, with coffee and cokes and a unisex restroom plastered with out-of-order signs we were still too naïve to know were lies.

What he kept calling around the curtain, from behind the camera, was that nobody was listening.

If it's possible to cry out your urethra, then that's what I did that day.

My dad, who wasn't listening, cheered and whistled and stomped in joy, and then it was Tandy's turn, which took fifteen minutes of muffled sobbing she'll carry with her to the grave, and then it was Roy's turn, which took exactly fifty-two seconds: he stood with his back to us and arced a line down to the waiting

John and pinched it off perfect, so not one yellow drop hit the floor.

After that it was the usual battery of oral quizzes on policy:

- what to do in cases where a colostomy bag and/or catheter was involved: This isn't discrimination, but we can't accept containers that don't have the Bladder Hut crest;
- what to do in cases of entrepreneurs or other franchise opportunities: use the Yellow Line and the proper series of code words ("sidewalk, cannery, Thomas");
- how to comport yourself if the health inspector's standing over your shoulder: "Exactly as you would if he weren't there, right?"
- how to cross whatever language barriers: it's a trick question. Relieving yourself is the universal language—"We're all metaphorically floating on generation upon generation of urine. We were born with these sea legs. These tides are part of us, and we're part of them" (Paternus Rectumis 24:7);
- what to do with a eunuch: that depends whether it's a free-range eunuch or not (none of us laughed at this—it's hard to tell between when my dad's joking and when he's just forgotten there are other people around);
- what to do with a suspected hermaphrodite: explain how our efforts to design a "Gene/Jean", that holy grail of the urine industry, have, due to certain anatomical issues, so far resulted only in complicated, whimsical devices.

My suspicion is that if you have to have a hermaphrodite policy, then you might just be in the wrong business.

Not to say anything bad about all the Genes and Jeans out there.

For all I've been able to tell, I mean, Prudence could be one.

But I'm not thinking about her.

Three hours to go.

One hundred and eighty minutes.

To kill time I fill in blank suggestion cards with outlandish ideas and insane business proposals—the only one in my own hand has to do with the long-term psychological advantages of using a more opaque plastic for the bottles, but I've been writing that every day for weeks already—each of which my dad will have to consider for a moment, maybe even look up in the index of his small businessman's handbook.

Is it actually feasible to have dogs help with disposal, or would there be animal rights involved?

Would hunters really be interested in purchasing gender-specific spray bottles of urine?

Should we offer a Free-Pee coupon to anyone able to fill three Johns or Janes in their allotted fifty-two seconds?

It's his fault Mom's wherever she is tonight.

I take my completed cards to the bay, drag the towel off the leaky plug and let the stream splatter the suggestions. This is just to make them look authentic.

I pen one more before walking them out to the box, in a hand I've been forging since elementary: my mom's.

And no, I don't wash my hands after.

20.

Three customers later—a pizza delivery guy from a place I'll never eat at again, a random businessman who takes a tie clip but doesn't put it on, a cop from a town whose colors are blue and darker blue—my dad's Sunday school class pulls up in the church van.

"You just missed him," I say, leaning forward, my arms crossed on the counter, hands hanging down into space, so casual.

Because of the goggles, to look at each of them requires more neck action than usual.

It's worth it, though.

They do not want to be here.

I lick my lips to keep from smiling, taste something pungent and bitter, then have to concentrate on breathing for a few seconds.

"You okay, son?" Mr. Walker calls from the passenger seat.

"The fumes," Edith Sarengen leans up to explain, her delicate hand on the back of Mr. Walker's arm.

Old people always hang onto you when they talk.

Otherwise you might get away.

"Been a long road," Mr. Healy explains from behind the wheel, leaning back to pat his stomach. It's maybe supposed to indicate a full bladder. For all of them.

They're not here because Dad missed choir practice or because there's another committee meeting or because the second service is becoming too much of a rock concert again. They're here because the tires on Dad's new car—he bought the Camaro almost specifically *for* the grand opening—they're from Mr. Walker's store. And the drywall we had to have put in, Rachel Raines' son got that one. Not because he had the lowest bid or had ever done anything like a good job, but because he needed the work.

Rachel is in the third row of seats, her hands in her lap like two dead fish.

There are empty coke cans and six-pack rings all over the inside of the van. They're not left over from the youth camping trip either, or from whoever's bowling night.

The Sunday school class has been cruising for hours, it looks like. Getting tanked on cokes. Talking themselves into this. Stopping so the women can duck into their houses, change into the most billowy skirt they own. So the men can migrate to the front of the van, just stare straight ahead.

We're going to need the backup glove, I'm pretty sure.

I might even have to ask them for some customer testimony, so we can feature them in the next round of brochures.

Do you mind if I take your picture, Ms. Edith?

Just hold it up like—yes, perfect, thank you.

You've done this before, haven't you?

I don't offer them any curtains.

21.

The before-dinner crowd is thin, as always. Especially with the Cockfight looming over the city. The Woodpeckers are the Bantams' mortal enemy. Sitting in the stands, all the fans' hats beaked, every last person screaming, it's easy to forget that sometimes.

Maybe an expert bird-watcher can tell the difference in the foam beak/brim of a woodpecker and the foam beak/brim of a chicken, but that's not where you look first in the concession line: Woodpecker jerseys are black and pale pink, while Bantam jerseys are deep green and bright white.

My Bantams hat is in my trunk, just in case.

It's a memento now, practically.

It's probably pregame right about now. For Chickenstein and the die-hards, and all the minors who slink up before security gets there, so they can drink.

This was supposed to be my year to be one of those minors.

In the milk tray by the second window are five Johns and four Janes. My dad's Sunday school class.

The part of me that's already been hell-bound ever since Prudence let me reach up under her shirt wanted to stand at the window as Mr. Healy was pulling them away, wave, and thank them with my best customer service nod. Say something along the lines of how our night shift attendant would appreciate their generous contribution. He definitely would.

And, did they know about the buoyancy properties of urine? I don't know.

I'll let my dad deal with his friends' pee. I push it to the back of the rack, scribble "holy water" on its dry-erase tag.

As for why I didn't say that about Roy, it probably had something to do with Rachel Raines in the back of the van, dabbing the corners of her eyes with a tissue and trying to smile, trying just to look ahead into this, the second part of her life.

I walk back and forth, window to window.

This is what my dad does, too, under stress.

Finally, because the lollipops in our salvaged pickle jar are just lollipops, no urine theme, no special shapes or wrappers, no tie-ins, I take two. Dinner. I ravage them, shred the sticks after the candy's done, leave the door open when I'm peeing and wash my hands so hard that water splashes everywhere. Then I go back to the bay and kick the plug of #1 until even my shoe hurts, but there's too much pressure, and then I hold the hair at the sides of my head like a character in a cartoon and I close my eyes and I *don't* cry.

Below me, in whatever used to be the pit before this was Rocket Burger, I can hear the pee dripping down from the rusted drain grate.

When I heard it earlier, waking up, aware of the rhythm before I even knew it was a rhythm, I could almost tell the moment a drop let go of the iron, plunged down to whatever dark, oil-coated sea is pooling down there.

Then—this was an hour ago maybe?—there was a definite second, maybe a second-and-a-half of free fall.

Now, splashdown is almost instantaneous.

In my head, I can see stalagmites and stalactites of urea forming in the old pit. A vast, yellow cavern. Fingers of translucent crystals reaching for each other from the floor and ceiling, every-thing wet, glistening.

It makes me cough.

Back when Tycho Brahe was alive, wearing a metal nose to parties, trying to pick up Renaissance girls with his knowledge of the night sky, the scientists of the day were still trying to extract gold from human piss.

The reasoning was that it's got to be that color for *some* reason.

I'm surprised they even had the wheel.

Not that I don't live with one of them.

22.

Darkness brings the jokers out.

Like my dad says, their money's as good as anybody's.

What I am is the lame zebra, watching the lionesses pace back and forth, casing the herd.

Keep moving, I tell them in my head.

Nothing to see here.

It's like I'm wearing a target, one I painted on myself, because of the church van.

I don't call the cops on the Yellow Line when a carload of guys I know by sight stop to pee on the thick metal base of our sign, and there's nothing I can do about the people driving by with their bare asses out the window.

Like with the Planned Pregnancy condoms, I'm not sure how mooning is really any kind of slam on a place that processes urine—some kind of toilet-eye view?—but maybe I'm not supposed to get it.

Soon everybody'll be at the game, though, screaming their throats bloody, and by the time they get out, they'll be Roy's responsibility, can pee all over the building for all I care, until it floats away.

And there's nothing I haven't seen anyway.

This is a hopeful statement, understand.

In the next thirty minutes, The Bladder Hut makes a clean forty-two dollars, hardly any of it on Upsales.

It's not minivan moms in the emergency lane anymore, but people I know from school, who move in packs. One of them, a girl named Karla, asks if I've done my geography yet.

I take her Jane, give her her change, and nod to the counter beside me, like I'm doing it right now, between customers.

I wonder if this means she won't want to borrow it in study hall?

Like me, it has to be contaminated by now.

That's what this woman told me early on, through the second window, right after she'd handed me her pee: I was going to get amoebas.

In lab at the school the other day, Mr. Lynn had to cup his hand around his mouth and call back to me three times to get my attention.

I was studying my hand under an ultraviolet lamp.

Greg Baines, who I couldn't hang out with anymore even if he didn't remind me of myself—he moved up to McKinney in eighth grade, is probably a hick now—I remember passing one of his dad's football cups back and forth over the toilet, so we could each fill the tanks of our waterguns. And I remember seeing for a moment how intense he was about it, and how unafraid he was about the water we were touching. How he was excited, almost.

His dad was a plumber.

That's how I explained it to myself. He had a resistance, he'd been born into this.

But no, I never stayed for dinner at his house.

The food, I always imagined, it would taste different. Wrong. Like his dad cut the carrots, or had touched the pitcher of tea right where it pours out. Had his hands all over the kitchen, probably.

I'm not a good person.

One of the cars passing by in the far lane over and over is Mark Broyles.

I think his car is what inspired my dad to get his.

Mark's is the ragtop version. Like everybody else, he's been through the drive-through once, just for fun.

Not like everybody else, he had a camera checked out from the A/V room.

Since he blew his knee out trying to save homecoming for us all, he's become the official chronicler of his junior year.

What he looks like with his stiff leg is a walking mannequin, his hair made of plastic, his face and shoulders designed by committee.

He's not coming through my drive-through, though. Yet.

It's just as well. I haven't had time to roll out the red carpet.

But then I remember that his mom is supposed to be in the book club with my mom. I remember her mentioning something once about "nice Mrs. Broyles." About her coffee.

This would mean she's really been over there.

I start watching for Mark's red Firebird to make the drag again.

While the cars stack up I clamp the Yellow Line between my shoulder and ear, call Prudence.

It breaks a promise I've already made to myself, but this is different: I'm not calling to check up on her, but to ask if my mother's car is across the street. Where Mark lives.

She's not answering, though. This is precisely why I promised myself not to call.

Now they're starting all over again, my thoughts.

What I want to say to that chauffeur is that no, you can't drown in your own goggles. Because the tears all go down the back of your throat.

I'm sure he's up in some skybox at the coliseum right about now, the sole of his right shoe pressing into Roy's throat, Roy's face pressing into the floor, where a pool of yellow is forming from a spilled plastic bottle. Cybil Leon and her people all sitting around with champagne and smiles.

I know how he feels.

23.

This is the joke I live in: Guy shows up all harried and nervous like he's just off work, and places a clear plastic cup on the ledge of the first window. It's one of those plastic cups with hash marks for milliliters, and it's got a fitted lid, and it's full.

A urine sample.

This is what the guy says: "It's clean this time, man. Promise. I need to sign something?"

The music in his car is blaring, not KPEE.

"We're not the clinic, sir," I tell him.

The "sir" is policy, in case this is another test.

This guy isn't my dad dressed-up. My dad's disguises are much more elaborate, and usually involve accents.

"What? Think I'm stupid?" the guy says, turning his radio down. "I *know* where the clinic is, man. That's where I did the paperwork."

"I'm just saying."

"What?"

"I don't—this is The Bladder Hut."

"And this is from my *bladder*," the guys says, lifting the cup just to set it down again.

The foam that's collected at the top is indistinguishable from the foam that rises from cooking macaroni.

There are so many things I don't eat anymore. Whole food groups. My third-grade teacher would be disappointed in me.

I know because I think she came through last week.

The reason I think that instead of know it is that for those fifty-two seconds and forty-nine cents, I was just two arms, reaching up from behind the counter, trying to toss a Jane through the window, then, at the second window, waiting, palm out, for her to throw it back.

I'm not a proud person. Pride has no place in customer service. This is gospel at Drive-Through U.

I try another angle with this guy: "It's against store policy for us to accept containers that don't have our seal on them."

This stops him for a moment.

"You mean—you mean you can like buy one of these piss-pot things, take it with you, fill it up, then return it?"

I look over his roof, to an irregularity in the wall of the building next to us.

Some days I think the irregularity is a place I've burned with my eyes. It looks different at night. Deeper.

"Not really, no," I admit. It's bad wording on my dad's part: we can't accept *any* containers, really.

"Then just, I don't know. Like, *pour* it into one of your sealed things, yeah? Or do you like have to *see* it come out?"

I look farther away, to a sharp red car that's not a Firebird.

"We're not affiliated with the clinic," I tell him. "We're more like a public restroom."

The headlights are piling up behind him.

"But you have to pay, like over in Paris or wherever?"

"Like in Paris, yes. Exactly like in Paris."

"What do they call them over there? 'WC'? 'Hold on, Charlie. I've got to take a slash in the WC right quick here.'"

His attempt at a cockney accent reminds me of Roy for some reason.

What I hope is that his urine is being tested to see if he gets to breed or not. Or for lava. That's it: I hope he has some STD that makes him pee real and true lava.

It would turn to black pellets of rock as soon as it hit the water. The rocks would ping against the porcelain, like chimes.

It's a sound I could get used to.

"No, it's 'loo,' right?," the guy's saying now, squinching his nose up in something like thought. "'Hold on a second, Charlie old matey, I've got to step into the *loo* for an moment here.'"

Lou's Place was a possible name, early on.

Not "Wash Closet," though.

That's stranded somewhere back in history, along with "toilet water" for perfume, and we're a *modern* establishment. It says so in the brochures.

If I could take a pill not to know any of this, I'd have overdosed months ago.

But the sample cup of urine is still on the ledge outside the first window.

I could give him a clean bill of health, I suppose, even sign it on Bladder Hut stationery to make it look right. It'd just be a visual inspection—no, I don't *see* any joints bobbing around in there—but it would satisfy him, I think.

Except I'm not touching that cup.

Not even with my gloves on.

"Do you want a John, sir?" I ask, holding one up. "We've got to move the line here, I'm sure you understand."

My idea is that, while he's being pulled forward to the second window, maybe he'll think *he's* supposed to just pour his sample into the jug. Maybe that's how these drive-through urinalysis joints work.

I'm even willing to pay the forty-nine cents myself.

This is a joke, though. My life, I mean. And that's no way for a joke to end. Who would laugh, right? Me, sliding quarters up from my pocket, two-fingering them into the register.

That's tragedy, not comedy. Prelude to a suicide. A cafeteria shooting spree in germ form.

"So you're saying you can't take my sample?" the guy says, leaning up out of his car more than I'm completely comfortable with. "Am I hearing you right?"

The THESE PREMISES ARE MONITORED signs only apply to the unisex restroom.

My hands are gripping the counter on my side.

Two more hours.

I nod, my lips together.

"What?" the guy says, still leaning forward, which is when I see the red eye of a cassette recorder glowing in the chest pocket of his shirt.

He wants me to *say* it.

"No, I'm sorry, sir," I clearly enunciate, "like I said, we're a commercial establishment. Not a medical one."

Across the street now, I see the car I should have known was going to be there, the guy leaning out with a video camera, the lens flashing at us.

He's already laughing.

Unless he has image stabilization, this is all going to be too shaky to watch.

That doesn't feel much like revenge.

I come back to the guy at my window.

"Well," he says then, taking the cup, peeling the lid off, "shit, man. I mean, if *you* can't take it, I'm just going to have to save it, right? Right?"

I nod without really nodding.

The guys shrugs like that's all the permission he needs.

"Well, back inside, guys," he says, lifting the cup as if to make eye contact with his pee. "We'll find somewhere, don't worry.'"

He says that down into the cup but also into his pocket. And then he drinks it all, so that it dribbles down his chin and throat, even.

It's beer, or apple juice, or anything.

Not urine.

He's laughing so hard he sprays the inside of his windshield, snaps his fingers to me for a wipe, a wipe.

I charge him four dollars for it, then go back to staring at my place on the wall of the building across the way.

I expect it to start smoking any minute now.

24.

I see Mark coming for a long time before he gets here. He's eighth back in line, and I'm slinging pee like I was born to it. I stare at his sloped hood and do the math in my head: fifty-two seconds times seven, plus the Upsales I'm supposed to make, minus the Upsales I'm not even going to try to make. So, fifty-two times seven. Then I can ask him if his mom kicked him out of the house tonight too, pretend that that's the only reason I'm here.

Mothers, what are you going to do?

We'll laugh, ha ha ha ha ha ha ha, and then he'll pass me a bottle of his urine.

At some point, working the line, I think I catch a dinosaur raising its head to see over all the cars—I'm so far past surprise now that if a fire engine showed up, needing Old Faithful and Annie to save the city, I'd shrug, nod, step aside—but then the dinosaur is just the beige top of Mark's Firebird, unfolding itself to connect with his windshield.

He's showing off, sure. Closing the door on what's about to be his restroom.

I clatter another full milk tray of piss into the tall cart and suddenly flash on taking a date through here. A girl. Me and Prudence, holding hands, taking our John and our Jane, still steaming from the dishwasher because The Bladder Hut's humming.

I could never do it, I don't think.

Not because of shyness—this would be even more intimate than talking about Poo Burgers—but because of things I can't really control.

The sign under our first window, like a caption under my face all day, is the kind you see at amusement parks before the roller coaster, about how this ride isn't recommended for people with heart problems, or pregnant women, or all the rest.

Technically, though, this isn't an amusement park

Our legal disclaimer is tailored for the urine industry.

It recommends that, if you're currently experiencing a persistent erection, then perhaps you should reconsider your visit with us today.

Our Johns aren't designed for hard-ons is the thing.

I mean, the mouths are wide enough, of course. But the only way to hit them even a little bit, especially with Prudence in the passenger seat pretending not to look—which is to say making everything worse—would be to back up a few steps, lean forward, and rainbow it on out there. Pray a little besides.

And in a car, even in a van, there's just not that kind of room.

And of course peeing straight up into the John, while that would keep your face dry, gravity would be working against you, and the date would be very much over.

As for lying sideways or even on your stomach if you have room, legally we can't endorse using our Johns in any fashion but the recommended fashion, which is with the base at a forty-five degree angle to your floorboard. And anyway, peeing shouldn't be a game of Twister. Especially on a first date.

Until the study was complete, my dad considered the benefits of making condoms available for the persistently erect to pee

into—maybe somebody at Planned Parenthood is telepathic?—
but the truth of the matter is that peeing into a rubber makes you
throw up a little, into the back of your throat.

No one will deny this.

So no, aside from that employees are forbidden from coming
through the drive-through like normal people, I could still never
bring Prudence here before the movies one night. It'd be like asking her to sit next to a sprinkler.

Never mind that the more I dwell on it, the less likely it seems
she'll ever be sitting beside me again. Because of one bad connection and one missed call.

Nations have fallen for less.

What I'm smelling isn't the fermented urine ankle-deep now
in the bay, but the carcass of our love.

And maybe, if I'm being honest, it started four months ago,
and isn't her fault at all.

I'd guess I'm less social than I used to be. More prone to fits of
shame and self-hatred. That I've been thinking entirely too much.
Talking to myself when other people are right there with me.

Maybe these are *my* dark years, yeah.

I mean, used to, in junior high and on into our freshman year,
I never called Prudence by her full name. It was always just "P."

The good old days.

I try to make a sound like a laugh, just to hear it, and hand a
John, a warm glove, and an overflow canister to the guy in the loud
pickup, number five before Mark.

Walking to the second window, I hear the pickup door open
and close, know there's another beer bottle out there now.

P.

I remember calling it across the gym once. It was the most innocent thing in the world. Prudence looked up, happy to see me,
then finished tying her shoe, her hair draped all around her, its
copper brown tips brushing the shiny wooden floor.

The vision changes, though.

Now the floor she's on is thick with wax that's gone yellow with age, and it's bubbling, rising into macaroni foam.

I push my goggles up, wipe my eyes with my sleeve, can almost taste the tang of overspray with my tear ducts, then slide the goggles back down, process the fourth car (either tag-team serial killers or two late-night elevator repairmen), the third car (college kids in a Jeep—three guys, three girls, five seatbelts), the second (a skinny man wearing obscenely short running shorts and nothing else, "for easy access," he says, patting his inner thigh), and then Mark's throaty Firebird is making the windows tremble.

I go to thread my bangs behind my ear but am wearing a hairnet. I play it off like nothing, jack a John up from its rack without asking. Because we're close like that, me and him; buds. I don't have to ask if he's male or female.

"Got to siphon the python," he says, already unsnapping, flaring his eyes to make his words rhyme.

"Shake the snake," I add.

Mark fingershoots me like I'm dead on here.

I lean forward onto my elbows, into this new friendship, and see that he's already got one of our curtains strung up beside him.

He sees me see it, reaches up to smooth the velcro to his roof a bit more.

"Must have forgot to give it back last time," he says.

It's one of the dark brown ones. It complements his interior well, I think, and comes down almost all the way to the console— close enough that the straws of the two drinks there are split. One's leaning over to Mark, one's his passenger's.

I lean back, suddenly ashamed for some reason.

I could never bring a date here, no, even though it'd be the next closest thing to actual sex, would maybe even count as foreplay, but it's no problem for him.

"Keys," I say, trying to be just business now, so I don't mess things up between him and her.

He smiles, passes them up, and something down near his shifter clicks.

It's his lighter.

We both look to it, and then to the curtain, the side of the girl's leg we can see through it.

She's sitting perfectly still, the way a chameleon will, but then the drink on her side rises from its cup holder, returns, and my world shatters, implodes, a light bulb too deep underwater.

The drink's a Purplelicious Rex.

"What?" Mark says up to me, following my eyes down to the drink.

I shake my head no, lurch back off the pedal, and his Firebird groans forward, my heart thumping slow and heavy in my chest, like it's dragging down, is just slushing my suddenly-cold blood around now, pushing it from chamber to chamber with no real plan.

Prudence?

Fifty-two seconds later I'm at the second window, my hand trembling, my mom a distant, distant memory, a mirage even, if that.

"All right there, champ?" Mark says, passing his John up to me.

Sport. Champ. Tiger.

My dad calls me all these things.

I take the John without even looking at it, let the silvery light of Mark's flash strobe me, lock me in place like this forever, his pee inches from my face, and now I can see fingertips on the purple drink. Nails painted a certain, certain way. Prudence.

Is this cheating?

Does sitting in the front seat with a guy while he's pissing into a bottle count, even if you look away, try not to hear?

Mark's saying something but it's muffled.

I blink, breathe, focus in on him.

He's holding two dollar bills out to me.

They're folded lengthwise.

I nod, take them, have forgotten the mechanics of swallowing. Somebody in line is honking—*that* registers—but I can't seem to process the sound, can't decode the horn, what it means.

"My mom," I finally manage to say.

Mark narrows his eyes at me, turns to question the curtain but it's just a curtain, those fingernails drawn back now.

"Gwen?" he says back.

I nod—yes, Gwen, Gwendolyn, this must be what I wanted, what I needed to ask him. I'd forgotten my mom's name and needed him to remind me.

"Thank you," I say then, for the name, the money, his pee, for just being him, then hand him his keys. He's already rolling his window up, as if there's a sea of yellow rising behind me and he doesn't want it flooding into his Firebird.

It's understandable.

I turn to at least see this tidal wave before it pulls me under, and in that instant Mark screeches away, and then I see why he wanted his window up.

Hissing in his urine, floating, is a lit M60.

There's about two seconds left on the fuse, I think. Just long enough for me to look into my other hand, to the two dollars he's paid me with, that he didn't want change for.

The top one has been smeared with crayons, like by a kid in a minivan.

It's a dollar Mark held his hand under the curtain for, I know, during that lifetime between windows. One of the dollars I gave Prudence, so she could buy a purple drink.

And the thing is, I don't know which is worse—that dollar in one hand, or the M60 in the other.

I smile the smallest possible smile, like I'm getting it at last, this joke.

Like it *is* funny.

And then the M60 sucks a cloud of urine towards itself at something like the speed of sound—I can *see* this—and my face starts to cup my eyes just a little bit, the first, useless motions of a flinch, and there's no time anymore, no noise, just this moment that won't click forward, this now, this well I'm standing in, looking up at the sky drifting over the world I used to know.

You could have heard a flea bark.

There are things so far
beyond belief that it
ought to be possible to
wake from them.
                    —DM Thomas

PART THREE

Leaktakers & Heartbreakers

25.

My dad could have had any number of other passions. He could have been into football and sacrificed me to his precious gods every Friday night. It would have made for some good Sunday afternoons. Him letting me hold iced-down beers to my knees so I'd be ready for practice on Monday.

Or fishing. If he was into fishing, we could have all the goofy hats and gear, and disappear every Friday with a cooler, and take pictures of each other holding fish after fish. These would be pictures I could show my kids in twenty years.

Or even cars. Then I could have a restored Mustang like Tommy Selznak, whose dad went so car-crazy that he only does his CPA stuff part-time now. The rest of the time he's out in his new shop, the click of a ratchet filling all the empty space, some bad old music coming from a shelf nobody can ever find.

I'd pay for that music.

Or he could just be like the rest of the dads: no dreams at all anymore. Just resigned pretty much, a look in their eyes like they're waiting things out here, and a sneaky smile that they remember being like you, sure. But wait a few years, kid.

You don't want to get trapped in a living room situation with those dads, no, but they tend to be pretty forgiving, too.

I don't know.

I'm just trying to come to terms with the warm urine beading on my upper lip, I suppose.

At least the world's finally quiet enough for me to think.

Thanks to Mark for that.

As for the John that was in my hand, it's gone—a water balloon lobbed into a rosebush.

My fingers are numb like you'd expect, but there's a cartoon feel to it all. Like I've still got the exact same posture. All that's changed is that I've been drawn in my exploded state now, though my hairnet's keeping my hair from spiking in the proper manner.

The pee misting through the air more than makes up for that.

Again, it's like I'm being given the chance to go back to the men's restroom of that Bantams game, save everybody from the poison urinal cake. Start over.

But I'm probably just trying not to be *here*, I'd guess. Not now and not for two more years. Twenty-four months. A pale yellow sea of days.

Will I still see Prudence in the halls?

Can I even ever go back to school again?

I can wash the pee out of my hair, but not out of everybody else's head.

Outside the second window, a girl from my grade's leaned up out of her mother's BMW. She's knocking on the window. With her *fist*, not a Jane. Like she's trying to save me.

I smile, shake my head no. Thanks, but no.

It's already too late.

According to my mom, who explained it to me in secrecy a long time ago, years before I was ready, the thing with my dad, the reason he's not into football or cars or math or fishing or pornography (I didn't even know what pornography was until this discussion), it all comes down to his name.

Instead of being a "Russell" like Tommy's dad or a "D.L." like Mark's dad or a "Weatherby Baines, III," my dad is a "Jan."

He often reminds us that John Wayne's real name was Marion.

According to my mom, who's paid a professional for it and evidently recites it to herself enough that it's become a chant of sorts, little boys with feminine names often overcompensate by fixating on male-coded activities. Football, science, or, in my dad's case, standing up to pee. Which he's been lucky enough to turn into a career.

That's not the word I would have used.

That my dad grew up in a household of women just contributes to this bladder infection of the mind. He was the only one who ever had to lift the lid, and was probably asked to conform to the rest of the house—to do "sit-down tee-tees" until his aim improved.

Studies have shown that that's never, though.

My mother laughed at this last part, I remember. A trilly, nervous sob of a laugh, like people do at funerals.

At the time I thought this maybe was another devious way to get me to be more careful in the bathroom—the "my aim is to keep this bathroom clean, your aim will help"-placard on the wall wasn't quite doing the job.

After talking to Roy, I have to wonder what it was during those dark years that drove my mom to seek professional help like that.

I mean, the porn she cued me into, it's been an education. The first time my dad showed us the sacred tablet of "Golden Rain Checks," I laughed a little through my nose before remembering that none of this was funny.

The one story I hope my mom didn't have to tell her professional help, though, because then I have to imagine my dad and her behind closed doors, with rubber sheets and an elaborate system of bedside gutters, is the one where my dad's visiting his cousins, swimming in their "(p)ool," and surfaces after some dive to gasp air, but still can't breathe.

What's happening is that his older cousin is standing with his back to the house, so he can pee on my dad.

It used to be my favorite gross-out story.

I'd make him tell it over and over, him miming the pee hitting his face, how he kept wiping his eyes, how he didn't understand at first, just kept trying to blink the water away.

I'd sit over in my side of his car and laugh and laugh and shake my head no, that that was the worst thing ever, *ever*, and then he'd flap his lips like making bubbles, shake his head to clear his eyes, and I'd scream with glee and hold my ears and pull my knees up to my face.

So we have that instead of football.

And I can't run anyway.

Things have a way of working out, I suppose.

26.

"Occupational hazard, son?"

This from the cop who thinks I should be flipping burgers.

His response time was nine minutes, because everybody in line had to get out of KPEE range for their cell phones to work.

This is going to be on the evenings news, I know. A pretty field reporter asking rhetorical questions: Was this inevitable? Is it all fun and games until somebody gets their eyes peed in? Should Bladder Hut management call for paramedics or for the plumber? And what of the real victims, those unfortunate people mired in line, the next restroom a whole mile down the road? Should Bladder Hut institute some policy that, if you're in line for more than five minutes, we supply you with complimentary seat pads and air fresheners?

I live at the circus, yeah. Come see me at the freak tent, my booth's easy to find.

Maybe I'll do that thing again where you can't tell if I've got football player pee on my face or if I'm crying.

Throw change if you want. Everybody else does.

I swallow, catch myself about to touch a spot on my cheek, to see if it really itches or if I'm just thinking it does.

Where I'm sitting for my interrogation is on the counter be-tween windows, the officer to my left, his notebook out like he doesn't want to miss a single word here.

He's just back from our PISO MOJADO bathroom, the tank back there still filling. From the smile on his face, I think he's feeling like he got away with something there. Stole forty-nine cents he wasn't going to have paid anyway.

I don't know if his hands are clean or not.

I focus past him, to the hall, try to make it a real casual move-ment.

The floor there's still dry.

Good.

I can't let him stand there much longer, though.

When his lights flashed blue and red on the glass, announcing that there was nothing going on here, I pulled the metal door to the bay closed.

Because Rachel Raines' son Chris was on meth the day he set that door, he did it perfect over and over and over, until it seals like a hatch. You can feel your ears pop a little when you open it.

So yeah, it's a temporary fix for the leak in #1, Old Faithful.

But my shift's almost over, too.

Like my dad says, hourly wages get an hourly work ethic.

He's usually talking about Tandy there.

"Occupational hazard," I repeat back to the officer, faking a smile I know he doesn't buy.

"We'll need your tape," he says.

"Tape," I say, as if tasting this foreign word.

"*Security*," he says, waving to the idea of the cameras in the drive-through. "We'll pull their plates, be waiting for them when they drag ass in tonight."

"After the game," I add, not looking at the back of his notebook anymore. "What'll it be?"

"Criminal mischief, vandalism, whatever we make stick? To them, I mean. Public urination? Did they pay, even?"

The crayola dollars.

I nod, suck my cheeks in.

"There aren't any tapes," I tell him. "Those are dummy cameras."

The officer stops writing, studies me.

"We're not a gas station," I say. "Drive-offs aren't a problem. And I've got their keys anyway."

"But not this time."

"I gave them back."

"Because they paid."

That sounds right, yeah.

"Drive-by Urination," he says then. "That work, you think?"

I fake another obviously fake smile, hold it until the officer sneers.

"Guess we'll need a description from you then," he says, disappointed. "Make, model—how many were there?"

"Just one."

"Male, right?"

"John."

"So you knew him?"

It's so hard to keep up.

I close my eyes, open them.

"There was just one *John*," I tell him, reaching over to tap a John on the counter, one of the ones filled with yellow wax. I think it's supposed to be a decorative candle, but have never asked.

"Then that means the perp was *male*, right?"

I nod.

"And you *didn't* know him?"

I collect all the spit in my mouth, make myself swallow it. Shake my head no, just once, like I'm being paid to lie.

The officer stares at me, not writing anything.

He's been lied to before, I suspect.

"Make, model?" he says, though his heart's not really in it anymore.

"Jeep," I say. "Or something with a...like a roll bar, I guess. It had decals all over it, I remember. The roll bar."

The officer watches me as if letting me reconsider this, then flips his notebook closed.

"One guy of indiscriminate age—"

"Twenty-five."

"—in a Jeep or a Bronco or a Land Cruiser or a Scout or a—"

"Chinese, too," I add, staring him down about this.

"That would explain the firecrackers," the officer says, not really playing along. "Maybe we should talk to management about it, think?"

"I'm the only one here."

"Your old man runs this place, right?"

I'm staring at the wall across from me.

"What say we call him?" the officer shrugs. "See how he feels about this destruction of property?"

"It's nothing."

"Nothing."

"I'm not even the one that called you."

"This can't be good for business."

"People still need to pee."

He snorts appreciation, doesn't disagree.

But he's not done with me yet either.

"Since you know everything," he says, dragging it out, "I guess you know you can't return to your, um, duties until the bus gets here."

My heart stutters just a little bit, my eyes widening in fear.

Bus?

"Ambulance," the officer explains, his eyes flat. "Medics have to okay you, being a minor and all. Working in these unsanitary conditions."

"We're up to code."

"*Were*, more like."

"I'm okay."

"And the city's liable if I leave you without making sure of that."

"Who's going to work the window, then?"

"I'm sure your old man'll understand."

I close my eyes. Somewhere in the city my dad's lurching from public restroom to public restroom. In between he's in his car, leaning down close to the seat to slam another fake beer. Every bar he walks into, his eyes are already watery.

What he's doing is guerilla marketing.

It's chapter seven in the yellow bible in his head.

I know because he took me with him once.

In the pockets of his slacks and stuffed into every pocket of his jacket is a urinal cake he's had stamped with our name and address. He calls them "breath mints for the toilet" and says that he's doing a service, really, replacing old cake with new. That the other merchants should thank him.

This doesn't keep his picture from getting posted on various cash registers and bulletin boards all over town, however, along with the bad check-writers.

To keep the other owners from replacing his cake with the one he's lifted out with his special tongs, he usually puts the old cake in the sink, crushes it down to glittery sand.

The beers between stops are so he can have an honest reason to ask where the restroom is.

What this shows, I want to tell this cop, is devotion to his business. Enough to risk bodily harm, maybe even a night in jail.

All of which is worthless if his business isn't even open.

But of course I can't say any of this out loud.

I shake my head no to the officer, that my dad won't understand. Not even close.

"Oh, I get it," the officer says back. "He'll get all 'pissed off,' right? That it? Pissed *off*?"

I smile like this is the first time I've ever heard this.

27.

Tandy's way of saying she's going to smoke out back by the suggestion box is that she's got to go "nicturate."

The first time we all heard her say it was a Saturday morning,
and my dad's ears kind of perked up. Something canine about the
angle of his head.

Micturate is the fancy way of saying you're peeing.

Nicotine is the active ingredient in cigarettes.

It took me a few moments to get it.

The way Roy announces he's going to smoke is to look around
as if counting heads then come out with a loud and gruff "Burn
em if you got em."

What I say is nothing.

Because I don't smoke.

Some Saturdays, Drive-Through U. can take three or more life-
times to get across.

Others, though—that first one anyway, when Tandy knew we
were still processing her *nicturate*, not yet sure it wasn't something
feminine—I like to think that as she was walking away she was
smiling, and that that cigarette she smoked out back, her elbow

riding her gut, her heel lodged in the stucco, her eyes fixed on the horizon, it was the most perfect cigarette ever.

If she's anything like me—and by the way she answers the phone, just listening, as if suspicious and bored all at once, I'm pretty sure she is—she ashed into the suggestion box that morning. Our first comment, and maybe the best.

"Where's your dad?" she says, in answer to me asking if she can come in for twenty or thirty minutes, until the ambulance clears me.

"Out," I tell her, because Officer Spinrad is standing there.

"What about P-Man?"

"P-Man?"

"Roy."

"Roy's at the game."

"I thought you were the one who liked hockey?"

"I can't really talk right now, Tandy."

Silence. The staring-at-nothing kind.

"You're on the Yellow Line?"

"Yeah."

"And your dad's really not there?"

"He's on, y'know, patrol."

Officer Spinrad flashes his eyes over. I shake my head no.

"You can have my cigarettes," I say into the phone.

"You'll smoke them all before I get there."

"I'll come up before school, spray the walls for you."

Another silence.

"All week?" she asks.

"All week," I tell her.

"Okay," she says.

Her voice is the kind of dead that makes me wonder if she starts shooting heroin right *after* her shift, on the way to the bus stop, or if she waits until she's actually on the bus.

Like my dad would say, though, using her as an example in Drive-Through U.: she's a trooper.

What he wouldn't say is that she's a trooper who's been marching all winter with no boots, and would now relish the heat of musket fire, and the sleep it offers.

I have an American History test Friday.

It's not really my big concern right at this moment, though.

Backed up all the way to the road are customers, some legitimate, their legs crossed under their steering wheels, some just here for the sideshow.

Forty-nine cents either way. Plus Upsales.

I comp two boxes of the expensive wipes, clean every crevice of my ear, every pore of my nose.

My clothes I just put in the curtain hamper, to cycle through the cleaners. I've got more in my locker. It's policy. My dad says that if you milk cows for a living, sometimes you get shot with the milk.

He's never even seen a cow, I don't think. The thrill in his voice when he says that—it makes me rub a spot on my temple sometimes. Makes me wish I didn't know some of the things I know.

"Want I should pass some of these bad boys out?" Officer Pettyman asks, spiraling a John up into the air, his hands an open clam under it, waiting to catch.

"She'll be here."

"She better."

Two minutes later, his John on the ground where he failed to catch it, Officer Spinrad goes out to unsnake the line—get the tail out of the road anyway.

I'm not sure if having customers out that far makes us liable for accidents or if it makes us a successful business.

I have until the ambulance gets here to smoke. Tandy was right. My lungs are thirsty, don't care at all what my mouth might be saying.

I sidle out back and light up, not holding the cigarette casual at all, but race-fashion.

Half a pack later, the air thick with horns, my eyes just slits supposed to make me look tough, a raggedy shadow takes form just down the wall from me, past the corner on the drive-through side, so that he's backlit by twenty headlights, his white hair glowing around his head, his wrists long and thin past the sleeves of his jacket.

I fumble my cigarette away, the cherry hissing into the pool under the air-conditioner, and try for the door beside me. It's locked. Of course.

"Cop says there's a box back here for correspondence," he creaks, taking a step closer to me.

The slot of the suggestion box is smoky with my ash.

I back just enough away.

He's not tall like he looked in the headlights. Old, though, maybe even ancient. And the jury's still out on whether he's the walking dead or not.

Just in case, I take another step away from the building, from the box.

This increases the number of directions I can run, should I need to. And I'm not disallowing straight up.

The old man rotates to keep me in his field of vision.

What he's holding is one of our brochures. Our genesis story one. And the *way* he's holding it—he's like the kid who gets a ticket to some magic place, but has had to fight through all these obstacles to get to that magic place. But at the end he's stumbling forward to the gate, ticket in hand, held up like he's been following it the whole time, to here, to this moment in time.

It's proof, I mean.

And the old man's nodding behind it.

"You're his son, aren't you?" he says. "The pee tycoon?"

I just stare at him.

He nods, answering for me.

"Makes you the pee *tyke* then, right?"

I'm still just staring.

"You give this to him," he says then, thrusting the brochure to me.

I take it because it means he'll pull his hand back to his side of the world.

"These are—you don't have to give these back," I tell him.

"I'm not one of your customers, sonny. I might even make you get a haircut when I'm in charge. Think on that, why don't you?"

He laughs, his eyes glittering, his dry tongue dabbing his purple lips, and then, instead of a graceful, spooky exit, he falls into some kind of coughing fit.

He has to reach out for the building to keep standing.

In doing so, he latches onto me, his skin like paper.

"Rumors of my—my…" he says when he can, but starts coughing again, just totters off, back to the old Lincoln he has to have parked out front.

I retreat to the other side of the building, peel open the brochure.

The part he has underlined in shaky pencil is the little headstone in the text, the name of the old fan who died from the poison cake.

Slipped in beside it is a clipping from the newspaper.

It's a retracted obituary.

Behind the clipping is a dark photocopy of the old man's driver's license, with all the numbers blacked out, and the names match—license to clipping. And the picture's the old man.

"Rumors of his death have been exaggerated."

That's the newspaper's joke.

I lower the brochure, study the building on the other side of us, that I never see.

When he's in charge here.

Because our whole business is built on his grave, pretty much. So what my dad needs is for him to stay dead, to stay quiet. To get the cut he's wanting, after whatever cut the urine overlords are already taking.

There's not going to be a pot left to piss in around here pretty soon.

My fingers twitch towards the idea of the Yellow Line, but the door's still locked.

And I'm not sure I want to call this emergency in anyway.

It could be my ticket out, I mean.

I'm not a good person.

28.

The waste management truck beats the ambulance to me by a clean forty seconds. Because the drive-through entrance is too clogged, the driver has to ease over the curb one wheel at a time, his left hand hanging on the air horn so that his truck is lowing like a cow, his smile wide in the windshield like he's saving the day here.

The drive-through line erupts, everybody flashing their lights and hanging out their windows and cheering.

Officer Spinrad rubs his nose so he can smile behind his hand.

Yeah, it's a big mystery, who would have the authority to call a truck like that here.

I rub my last cigarette out under my shoe, all the smoke in my lungs leaching through to turn my insides grey. At least according to the animated movies at school.

We've got maybe five minutes before the news vans circle in, I figure.

Free advertising. That's what I plan on telling my dad. A media event. "The owner's on vacation and the attendant is off his meds, is handing out Johns and Janes for half-price for a limited time!"

Prudence would have liked it, I'm pretty sure. Once upon a better time.

I'm about to start thinking about her all over again when suddenly Tandy's standing behind me, like she just parachuted in.

"You're spraying the walls down all next week, too," she informs me.

I nod, deserve this.

"You've got a key?" I say.

She flips the door open for me to follow her in.

When I don't she turns, the question there in her eyes.

"I've got to get checked out," I say, hooking my head over to the two trucks.

"Which one?" she says back, looking from waste management to the ambulance.

It's a good question.

I meet the paramedics out by the dumpsters.

"You the one?" the first guy says.

"...one they call the *whiz?*" the second adds, already shying away to laugh.

Comedians, good.

I probably wouldn't have known what to do otherwise.

"What do you need?" I say, my hands to my pants.

At this point, stripping down in the parking lot wouldn't even be an indignity. But all they need, as it turns out, is my heart and blood pressure and a penlight in my eyes. And to ask me if our overflow canisters really say *"for when your cup runneth over."*

More laughing.

I shrug, ask if they'd like a Golden Rain Check as a token of my appreciation maybe?

This slows them a bit.

"You've got them with you?" the second one asks.

"Even better," I say, and when I start to unzip my pants they push me out the back, leave me standing there.

Twenty feet to my left is the waste management guy.

He's in an environmental suit, his helmet cocked under his arm, his truck shiny and sharp behind him like a 1950s spaceship.

"I didn't call you," I say across to him. "It's a joke."

He lifts his eyes to The Bladder Hut, says, "No shit, man."

We're the same, me and him.

It's why I don't cross the parking lot to shake his hand. We already know each other as well as two people possibly can.

I take my clean bill of health around to Officer Spinrad. He doesn't see that the medics have written "Schlong Weasel" in place of my name, just shoves it in his shirt pocket, keeps directing traffic, his face red from blowing the whistle.

"Shouldn't you be sitting somewhere," I say, "watching me flip burgers?"

He waves a car past.

"Just keep talking, kid. Keep talking…"

The reason he doesn't finish is that some seniors in a pickup are trying to drag a construction site porta-potty across the street to deal with the line.

"I guess you don't know them, either," Spinrad says.

"Competition," I say, and he's off, doing his best imitation of a run.

The seniors abandon the porta-potty in the turn lane, fade into the night, a beer bottle actually spinning on the road behind them.

T-minus twenty seconds for the news, I'd guess.

My sweet romantic teenage nights.

Before going back inside, I try to peel my cigarette up from the ground for one last drag, and a hush falls across all the cars in line.

I don't even look up.

29.

Goldfish and alligators will grow according to the size of their containers.

I think about this more each day.

Because of Dick, yeah, moving from cloud to cloud of urine, but because of some other reason too that slips away if I think about it too hard.

It has to do with me, though. With all this.

The other day, alone before the five o'clock Friday crunch, without even thinking about it, just while I was delivering it back to the bay, I peeled back the lid of a fresh Jane a few steps too early, and—I can't explain this—I dipped my head a bit. To smell. And it took me a breath or two to realize what I was doing. Then I had to get the mop.

But it wasn't enough.

That taste is still in the back of my throat, the back of my mind.

Am I like him?

Is this how it starts?

The joke I make about him sometimes with Mom is that psychoanalysis for him would be a visit to the urologist.

I haven't followed it all the way out to wherever it ends yet, but it sounds funny anyway, gets me and my mom across whatever awkwardness he's left us in, and we laugh instead of cry, and that's good enough for now. This is how people live from moment to moment, I think. It's about getting by.

Except, lately, I haven't been getting by so well. My mouthwash sessions have been lasting longer and longer, and deep enough that I gag sometimes, and once I even threw up what I know was bile, but, still, it was yellow, and thin.

What I'm afraid of, I think, it's bigger than just me and him. It's about fathers and sons. How us sons are all in tanks, like, in bubbles of our father's hopes and dreams and mistakes and regrets, and how there's something in us that knows better than to stretch out too far, because there won't be any room left to move around then, and we'll burst the bubble, drown.

I think this is why my throat constricts sometimes when I'm standing behind the glass of the first window.

But I don't know. Anything.

It's easy to get weepy when you've got a brochure in your pocket that can make everything go away. You kind of start to miss it in advance. The good old days when you had something to hate besides yourself.

Used to—two hours ago?—this was the kind of stuff I'd save to tell Prudence.

She's probably what I'm really missing.

I'm not stupid enough yet to miss all that other stuff.

Just her.

30.

The porta-potty in the turn lane explodes ten minutes after I get behind the second window again. Everybody sees it: a sophomore in his dad's vintage Mustang locks his arms against the steering wheel, yells—all we can see is his mouth, open, but we'd be screaming too; it's the only way—then turns away at the last instant, the bright blue porta-potty leaning towards his windshield as if bowing to him, and then it holds that polite stance for maybe twenty feet until the base disconnects, tears out the Mustang's exhaust when he clumps and splashes over it.

The sparks sizzle out in the spilled contents of the base, of course.

Tandy looks over to me about it and I nod, understand. This'll be part of the stories people tell for ten years, probably. The legends. And we're part of it now. It happened that night—this night.

I take a warm John, rack it without looking, and start to hand the change back through the window but the customer's already gone.

Tandy's staying around just until the line's under control, she says.

With both of us working, that'll be in about fifteen minutes.

She's not even asking people if they want curtains. The darkness is their curtain. It's something she probably doesn't know, always working the early shift.

At one point she announces she's hitting the John.

I can't tell if this is a joke or not, so hold up an empty.

She smiles a tolerant smile, nods to her window for me to get the next car.

"Watch out," I call back to her. "Camera in there."

She doesn't need me to tell her, though.

On the way down the hall she runs her fingers along the molding up near the ceiling, comes down with a long, thin rod of sorts.

Skewered at the end of it is one of those rubber balls made up to look like an eyeball, so that I have to see her sitting on the toilet, pushing the eye against the lens of my dad's hidden camera.

Life doesn't always suck.

Fifty-two seconds later she's back, drying her hands on her pants, stepping up onto the pedal to stop the car rolling up to her window.

"You were going to give me your cigarettes?" she says.

I pretend not to hear her. Just to stare straight ahead.

She laughs a sick laugh through her nose.

When the Yellow Line rings she brings it back with her before the next car's to her window.

She listens, passes two Janes through the window then clamps the receiver between her jaw and her collarbone, calls over to me about whether we have truck parking or not?

She knows we don't. What she's really asking is if I follow policy even with my dad not here. Policy in the case of truckers is to strap on the heavy tray, walk out to their window like a carhop.

I shake my head no, please.

This makes her smile.

"Only Bladder Hut containers," she says into the phone, staring at me the whole time, and I wince just a little.

Tandy feeds the trucker our address, then gives perfect directions from the interstate.

"Thanks," I say, my lips pursed so I won't smile.

"He probably won't even show up," she says, almost laughing, too.

The thing is, nobody likes pee novelty more than truckers. To them, handing their Johns down from their tall windows, and me standing there waiting for them to hand it down, I don't know. It does something for them. They'd pay even more, I think.

Since an incident the first week, though—my dad with the tray, pulling himself up onto a trucker's running board with his hand on their mirror strut, and the trucker just happening to open his door at that exact moment—we're always to stand at least six feet away, at least until we've established eye contact.

Except that's probably part of the rush with the truckers: watching us watch them. Staring us down about it. Daring us to look away.

I've only ever had to do it once, but it was enough. Working the window, you're in a display case, more or less. But you get used to it, and feel naked without it, standing out in the parking lot. Like the trucker's going to need to punch some more quarters into the slot here.

Two of them to be precise, each exactly as warm as the John you're holding, but thinking about those kinds of things never helps.

They're customers, business. Part of the job.

And, according to my dad's books, if we can reel in the interstate traffic, then nothing can stop us.

I'm not blind to the way he lights up about the truckers.

His thesis is shut down, sure, but the big trucks swinging wide to turn in—if he could collect demographics from them that he could index with their samples, then his old professors would have to listen to him, right?

It might keep him from trying to slip through the drive-through while on patrol, anyway.

"Four!" Tandy calls out. It's how many bottles I'm supposed to collect from the car in fifty-two seconds.

I take them, nod thanks for the extra eleven cents and then stare at the inside of my goggles until the next car—"One!"—groans up.

Like always, I lean forward, my eyes fixed on the customer's roof.

The John the guy passes me is light. In it, a piece of laminated paper?

I snap a mental picture of him, study it while I peel the lid back: he's tall, graying, looks like an early morning jogger. A doctor, maybe.

But then the whole second window glows blue with ultraviolet light. Even some of my arm.

I look to Tandy, my mouth open, and then to the laminated paper in my hand.

It's an ID badge.

D.R. Collins, the Health Inspector.

He's waiting for me when I track back up to him.

"Hear you had a *situation* earlier," he says, his voice a cross between a purr and a growl, then sets his emergency brake, turns his hazard lights on, and unfolds himself from the car, pans all around as if seeing this alien landscape from an all-new angle now.

I swallow, my face hot. I can already hear Tandy below the counter, trying to call my dad on the Yellow Line.

30.

The shirt I'm wearing for the inspection is one of the freebies my dad Hail Mary'd into the crowd the day of Grand Opening. He had them made in four colors. Mine's grey, with bubbly yellow letters framed in cracked decal white: *I MADE WATER AT THE BLADDER HUT*. It's one of the ones somebody threw back.

I wouldn't be wearing it except, in a fit of hygiene two weeks ago, I already used my first backup shirt.

I'm only saying this because it seems to be important to the health inspector. Mr. Collins. *Dr.* Collins, Darth Collins, I don't know.

He doesn't have to narrow his eyes to read my shirt, I don't think, but he narrows them anyway.

Behind me, at the first window, Tandy is a robot. She can't even look over at us. The last thing she said before I opened the back door was that she wasn't supposed to be here. That she was supposed to be watching *Touched by an Alien*.

The Yellow Line is back in its cradle on the wall.

My dad never picked up.

Collin's face is neither kind nor accusing.

I think it's something he learned in some seminar, probably: how to look completely neutral. How to make his face into the bureaucrat's version of an executioner's mask.

He's holding a tackle box of insane equipment.

Tandy doesn't need to go home to catch her show. It's about to happen right here, I'm pretty sure.

"He doesn't make you wear the noses anymore?" he says.

I shake my head no. The noses are history.

"It was a firecracker," I blurt out then, balling my fist to slow my words down. "We're usually cleaner."

He smiles, focuses past me, to Tandy.

And then he comes back to me.

"Your father is quite the repurposer," he finally says. "Those were for bread, right?"

He's talking about the tall, wheeled racks we slide the milk trays into.

"Rocket Burger," he intones, smiling a little, studying the new ceilings. "Buns." A muscle jumps on my neck. I try to rub it back down.

"Don't know if you know this or not," he says, "but it's customary at…during inspections, to first have an off-the-record conversation with the senior employee on premises. To dispel any suspicions of ill will and allow the inspector to know about any special circumstances. Any *fire*crackers, as it were."

The way he holds his eyebrows up at the end of this means it's a question. An invitation. For *me*. Not that I'm more senior than Tandy—we each have the same four months of our lives to repress—but I am the proprietor's son. The acting manager, I suppose. The prince. And it's my shift anyway; Tandy's not even on the clock.

"A conversation," I just manage to get out.

In one of the Sunday comic strips, I forget which one, but I used to see it every morning before church, when my dad was digging through to be sure all his ads and listings were there like he'd paid for—whichever comic strip it was, the way the artist draws one of the kids, when that kid's nervous, is he just puts these parentheses around his eyes.

That's me, now.

"A conversation," he repeats slower, casting around for, I don't know, a breakfast nook we can step into. A study carrel. A refrigerator box. "So as not to suggest any impropriety," he continues, his voice exactly like a nudge, "this is usually carried out in some more public portion of the establishment."

Except the whole place is off-limits. Drive-through: public. In here: way private.

He can read this on my forehead, I think, and blinks once to remind me of the public restroom we have to maintain.

"It's out of order," I tell him. "Temporarily."

He cocks his head about this, looks through the walls at the unisex bathroom.

I step aside so he can see the out-of-order sign for himself.

He walks down to the hall, Tandy's back swaying away from him as he passes.

Instead of checking the bathroom off on his report, he notes it on his mental scratch pad.

It makes his face kinder, somehow. More satisfied.

"Not to be crude," he says then. "But your shift is five hours, correct?"

I nod.

"Where do you relieve yourself?" he smiles, almost a whisper, as if it would be disrespectful for him to let Tandy hear this. Mixed company and all.

Right now she's trying to pretend an ashtray hasn't been dumped in the John she's holding with the tip-most part of her fingertips.

As I watch, trying not to, a single, live .22 round slips out of the floating mat of cigarette butts, torpedoes for the bottom of the John, the urine swirling bubbly white behind it.

Collins clears his throat.

The Bladder Hut is his playground, I know. Where old health inspectors go when they die, if they've been good.

"That used to be the kitchen," he says, nodding down the hall to the bay door.

"Storage," I say. Instead of running off into the night, I mean.

I don't have his head-on view down the hall, so don't know if Chris Raines' meth-head door is leaking around the bottom edges or not.

In case it is, I already have the PISO MOJADO signs in place.

Maybe that'll help, I tell myself.

And then maybe a rainbow will light the way over to my car, too. A rainbow with just blue and green and orange and red and violet.

"Where do you suggest, then?" Collins says.

I can feel Tandy listening to us.

"Out back, maybe," I try. It's as far away from the bay as I can think.

He stares at me about this, calling my bluff.

I lick my lips, swallow, turn to a car in the drive-through that doesn't need my attention. They're honking at Collins' car.

He looks up at them with his pleasant face, but I see now it's the way a lizard looks at a bug: like he's got all day.

"Let me put my case up first," he says, lifting it to pat it. "Wouldn't want to set it on the ground."

"You could leave it in here," I offer.

He looks around at the counters of The Bladder Hut, his eyes probably fitted with ultraviolet lenses, and shakes his head no. Thanks, I'm too kind, but no, never.

I nod, understand, don't need ultraviolet contacts to know about any of the surfaces in this place, and he steps out, first tipping a hat he's not wearing.

Behind him, I'm just breathing, deep.

"What do we do?" Tandy whispers, then flinches back from her window.

Collins has just put his own sign up on the outside of our window.

TEMPORARILY CLOSED FOR CITY HEALTH INSPECTION.

"I'm sorry I smoked all the cigarettes," I tell her.

"Tomorrow. You can…give me some tomorrow," she says back, a new hitch in her voice.

I don't look over at her, just walk past, to the back door.

"Don't go in the bay," I remember to tell her, then do turn around, to catch her eyes, let her know this isn't a joke.

She nods, not a flicker of a smile, and I turn all the lights off, inside and out.

This innovative economic system reduces
major points of cross-contamination
and ensures that your Flushboy™ wall-
mounted lavatories are always clean
and presentable.
    —Autohygiene™ Owner's Manual

PART FOUR

The Gospel of P

32.

The health inspector is sitting on the curb that collars our twin dumpsters. And they're just dumpsters, like the utility pole's just a utility pole and the parking lot's just a place to put your car for a while.

My dad's one try at infecting the whole property instead of just the building was to start calling the drive-through tracks the "urinary tract."

He was the only one who ever said it. It wasn't that the name didn't fit, it was that it fit too well.

"So?" Collins says, when I'm just standing there.

It's an odd word, like we're already halfway into this.

He pats the spot of darkness to his left like a grandfather might, and I sit a little farther down the curb, my arms hugging my knees, a raw pink color spreading across the walls of my lungs, all the tar and nicotine in my body flushing out, abandoning me, stranding me alone in this nightmare.

What I'm watching just to keep from jittering is the drive-through window, for a Tandy-shaped form to roll out, ninja down the side of the building, fold herself into a shadow.

It's what I'd be trying to do. It's what I'm doing in my head.

This is the first time in four months The Bladder Hut's been powered down.

As my eyes adjust, I cue in that Collins' tie is looser than it was when he came through the drive-through. And that he still has his ultraviolet flashlight. It's just hanging there in his hands, his hands hanging from his arms, his elbows on his knees.

This is all supposed to keep me from having a heart attack, I think.

"I didn't wash my hands," I tell him. "In the bathroom, I mean. At work. Once."

Collins nods to himself, considers this.

"And you'd be willing to testify against yourself?"

"I don't have to confess. It's on tape."

Collins almost has to smile about this.

"You're not just trying to keep me from performing an inspection here, are you?"

"He's going to show it to you anyway."

"He?"

"My dad."

Collins reevaluates me some then goes back to studying the building. And breathing in his controlled way, like he's drinking the air through his nose. Like this is yoga class. We're sitting too close for eye contact's the thing. Like the way, at a wall of urinals, you just stare straight ahead.

"He would do that?" he finally says. "Turn you in even though it's contrary to his business plan?"

"He does his cost analysis Sunday mornings, if you know what I mean."

"In the offering plate, yes."

"Let's not get crazy, here."

He chuckles, I chuckle. It's a regular chuckle fest.

He was supposed to have bit on that security-tape gag, though. Big time. He was supposed to have let me throw myself on the tracks. Retire my time card and save my dad's life work in the same heroic action. Go down in flames, hero for the cause, all in the name of family.

It was going to be even more of a sure thing than the old man's brochure in my back pocket.

Except now we're talking about church.

"And what about you?" Collins asks, a glimmer in his eye I don't like at all. "Like father, like son? Do you like working here?"

"Do I like working here…" I repeat, tasting it.

"You're part of something," Collins says, as if I didn't hear him the first time. "No longer can we say restroom facilities are bound by conventional concepts like walls, or decency. Did you know there's even some people who believe that social roles are both assigned and reinforced at the urinal, at millions of urinals a day?"

I'm not looking at him now. Anymore.

He doesn't need permission, though.

"It's not a revolutionary idea," he says. "Biology, by making men stand to relieve themselves, is also conditioning their depth perception, their hand-eye coordination, honing their sense of cause-and-effect, everything they're going to need when aim becomes useful for hunting or for battle. The weapon's already in their hand, so to speak. And women are equally conditioned by having to sit down, of course. To nest, to invest themselves not in the product or effect of their urination, but the process, leaving their hands free. I'm guessing this isn't news though, right? This should all be first-hand for you."

He taps his forehead to indicate my goggles, my job. Not my gloves, like I was thinking.

"It's just peeing," I tell him. "There's nothing Darwin to it."

"But you will admit that men and women go about it differently?"

"Doesn't matter whether I admit it or not."

"A pragmatist. Good. That should make you easier to negotiate with."

"If you're trying to sell me something, we've got a sign around front."

No SOLICITORS. Collins doesn't laugh.

"I'm trying to *give* you something," he says. "Men stand, women sit. It's a fundamental difference that establishments like this, if allowed to proliferate, will eventually dissolve."

"Girls get Janes, guys get Johns."

"A negligible distinction in design."

"You ever tried to pee in a Jane?"

"Point taken. However, notice that, even with different receptacles, *everybody* in your drive-through is sitting down. What this contributes to is a—a certain homogeneity in wastewater elimination that could, if left unchecked…well."

I look over to him now.

"You do understand that we're just a coin-operated pee shack, right? An outhouse with a business plan?"

"And attendants."

"*Personnel.*"

"People who wish to be personnel, I believe they *apply* for that position, do they not?"

I force myself to laugh a little, in appreciation.

"If you're worried about keeping the streams from crossing," I say, "the men go in one tank, the women in the other."

Now it's his turn to laugh a little. He even adds to it by leaning his head back, studying the stars.

"There's a difference in separation and segregation, of course," he says, switching his light to his other hand. "But neither is the issue here. What I'm talking about is"—he looks over at me, as if to see if I'm ready—"it's larger. More encompassing."

I suck my cheeks in, shrug with my eyebrows.

From where I'm sitting I can see a little bit of the road.

Officer Spinrad is sitting on his hood, guarding the entrance, nodding to the one car that starts to pull in: yeah, they saw right, our lights are out. The Bladder Hut is temporarily out of service.

Please use the truck stop down the road.

People are already coming to depend on us. To expect us to be here.

Worse, I feel kind of guilty about just sitting out here.

"This difference I'm talking about is more essential," Collins says, leaning forward a bit. "Imagine if you will that—that all of humanity is one animal, one organism. One life. A molecule, in terms of the universe. A zygote."

"I thought we were talking politics."

"This is science."

"The science of pee, yeah."

Neither of us looks over now.

"So if we're all one organism," he says, hitting each syllable for me like a teacher, "what would these seemingly small differences in posture seem to indicate?"

"I going to need to know my horoscope for this?"

"The differences could be cell *differentiation*," he says, ignoring me, preaching now. "The initial divisions and specializations of *life*. This"—here he opens his hand to the sky; what I'm supposed to get out of it is "Milky Way," I think—"it could be our first nursery. A womb. What if we haven't even been born yet? What if all of human history has been a single heartbeat, or not even that, just one cell becoming two, waiting to *become* a heart?"

"Just what the universe needs," I tell him.

"If you endanger these divisions by artificially forcing one stream this way, one that way," Collins says, his lips sounding thinner, less patient, "these differences, just that slight historically unprecedented shift in pH returning to the ecosystem, then the whole human *race*, it could never get the chance to—"

"You *are* trying to sell me something," I cut in, standing so he can be sure about it. "And I'm not authorized to make purchases. I just take deposits. You're going to have to talk to my manager, I think."

"Your dad."

"My dad."

We stare into each other's eyes like gun-fighters at high noon. A bay door back there lapping with pee, probably. My mental trigger-finger itchy. Prudence is already at the game with a football hero, I mean, and my parents are splitting up, and there's urine in my hair.

What else can he do, really?

Put a Gatorade bottle of piss in my locker?

Get in line, Inspector.

"It doesn't matter whether you subscribe or not," he says, his voice a hissy kind of whisper. "At your age I likely would have been suspicious as well."

"You never had a job like this," I say to him, patting my pockets for the cigarette I know I don't have.

"They're all like this," he says, standing as well, and something inside me crumbles. Keeps crumbling.

They're all like this.

Tandy'll bum me a cigarette, I know. She'll see my face and she'll even light one for me, pass it across. I'm going to be spraying the walls down all year, probably.

That's feeling like a pretty even trade.

"So what now?" I ask, my finger jittery. "You shut us down, right? Public decency, all that? Preserve the species?"

He chews his tongue some before answering.

"Finding violations here would be child's play," he says, flashing his light on the ground then clicking it back off. It stains my vision blue, gives The Bladder Hut a ghostly tinge. "But I don't think that's what's called for here. Tonight."

This stops the nicotine fit my feet are having.

"If I shut this establishment down for health concerns," he says. "Another will spring up, cleaner, with more insidious coupons. And if I shut that one down, another..."

"Whac-A-Mole," I say for him.

"Whac-A-Mole," he agrees, miming it with no real heart.

"Then...what?"

"It needs to fail on its own. As an example to other entrepreneurs. To discourage subsequent attempts. An inherently flawed enterprise. So your father can get on to his next urinary venture."

"*Next?*"

Collins nods like here comes the sad part of the night. "That cake he's discreetly distributing around town right now, it's quality cake. He should pursue that. A man with his inclinations and drive, he might just end up with the city contract. If certain people call in certain favors."

This is another invitation. This is us negotiating.

Instead of handling the public's warm pee, I could be delivering boxes of bathroom supplies to local merchants, my goggles long retired. You can pay for college in a variety of urine-related ways. Of this I'm nearly certain.

"It's a secret family recipe," I say. "That cake."

Collins hisses a laugh out.

"It's taken him a while to develop it," he says. "But I wouldn't say 'secret.' We've been keeping tabs on your father's cake-related activities for quite some time now."

He looks over to me again, to see if I'm hearing this like he wants me to.

I don't think I am, sir. But I am looking hard at the side of the building, trying to track it: of course it took a while to develop. You don't just stumble onto the urinal cake formula while making waffles one Sunday morning.

"He mixes it in the garage," I finally say. "Has a special fan and everything."

"I'm sure he would invest in proper facilities if asked to deal in volume instead of prototype. Quit using muffin pans, as it were."

"Either way," I say.

"He's innovative."

"That's one word for it."

"But you will tell him about this?" Collins says, tracking Spinrad's deliberate, lights-off exit, falling in after a Camaro it hurts to have to recognize. "And then we can forget about any—any videotapes that happen to show up?"

I smile a bit, bringing him back to me. "What videotape?"

He nods back.

"The city, at current count, has nearly eleven-thousand urinals in operation. And each one of them needs a…what does he call them? Throat lozenges?"

"Lozenges are for proper drainage," I recite. "Not freshness."

"Of course," he says back. "He already has the product line in place, and the dim shape of a branding campaign. I would expect no less from an entrepreneurial mindset such as his. Perhaps he'll see that there's a little more dignity in maintaining rather than abusing public hygiene."

I shrug.

"Just in case, though," Collins says, and somehow has a urinal cake in his hand.

It's in a plastic baggie, so it isn't new. There's no stamp on it either.

"This could be anybody's," I say, taking it by the highest corner.

"Except it's not," Collins says, and leaves it at that, suddenly cranking his head over: trotting up, its tongue lolling, is a stray dog. Its ears perk up when it sees us, and it swerves around the dumpsters, stops at the building, and lifts its leg right under the suggestion box.

Comment #2.

I cup my hand around my mouth and call out "Forty-nine cents!" after it.

In the silence afterwards, Collins is studying me.

"What?" I say.

He shakes his head no.

"*What?*" I say again.

He scrapes his top teeth over his bottom lip.

"It's not enough," he says. "Forty-nine cents."

"We make our money from Upsales."

"'Recreating the experience,' yes."

He's quoting our brochures.

"It's like he *wants* to be caught," he adds, a tinge of pity rising in his voice now. "Is that a religious impulse, you think? To turn him*self* in? Or is he taking the bullet for you, as it were? Is it an act of love, I mean?"

"I don't—he handles disposal every Saturday, if that's what you're saying. It's legal. It's not about love, I don't think."

"Have you seen him do it?"

I don't have an answer. I'm not even that sure what the question is. That my dad's in bed with some Porta-John Godfather?

Again, we fall into a shrugging kind of silence.

Finally Collins breaks it by flipping his light on, the beam shining up from between his knees.

The dog's pee is a deep throbbing blue against a background of older pee, and above, at about eye-level, high enough that, to pee there, somebody would have had to stand on the roof of their car one night after his shift, are letters making words. In the drippy, splattered cursive of urine. It should be unreadable, except, well. Guess you had to be there.

I cry freely.

Collins holds his light there long enough for the words to burn into my eyes, words he's known about the whole time we've been sitting here, then he sucks the light back in, pats me on the shoulder, and stands easier than a fifty-whatever-year-old dude should be able to, walks neatly to his car, looks back once to tip the hat he's still not wearing.

What we're supposed to do if the health inspector's around is what we would normally do, I know.

For the next few minutes, normal is sitting on the curb back by the dumpsters, my arms wrapped around my knees, a urinal cake in my hands that's rounded off on the edges, like a breath mint someone's been sucking on for a few days, or weeks.

Maybe even four months.

33.

Because the Cockfight's gearing up, the streets are empty when I turn the lights back on. Tandy's gone, of course, I don't know how. The Bladder Hut sign sputters for a couple of minutes then catches, all the moths cooked off.

I stand in my window and don't call Prudence, don't want to hear the game behind her.

I liked it better when the drive-through was stacked with pee, I think.

I crank the window open, count six cars passing, then crank it closed again.

Another name my dad wanted was *#1 Stop*.

The reason he didn't use it, finally, was that he wanted to save it for when we branched out into selling burgers at one window, taking pee at the other. Travelers would never have to get out of their cars then.

He calls this the American Dream.

Until somebody's order gets mixed up.

As for Roy, his dream isn't that much different, really.

I don't know how much he can make off Cybil Leon's Jane if he gets it signed, but it'll be something. Maybe enough to finance the rest of his study, keep him swimming in urine for years to come. Golden showers, yellow baths. I wonder if, floating in it like he does, you even notice if you start peeing yourself? The warm spot is already all around you.

It might be mystical, like he says. No clear line between what's inside you, what's not. Just a continuum of warmth.

The womb, yeah.

Maybe him and Collins are more alike than anybody knows—each just versions of the guy who used to always wait to get in line behind single women, then offer me twenty dollars for their Janes. Then forty. Then ten just to *see* which one was hers. Twenty more if I'd promise to pour his into hers while he watched.

For a week or two he was buying all Prudence's purple drinks.

Those weren't the good old days, though. Just more stupid ones.

I put Tandy's sign up, sit on the floor beneath the counter and ferret one of Roy's half-smoked butts from the wads of gum he sticks them to when a car pulls up.

The Yellow Line saves me from infecting myself with that butt.

It's the trucker Tandy gave directions to.

"You the jack-in-the box I'm looking for?" he says, so that I can hear him grinning, practically.

I stand in my window, my box.

The trucker's parked out past the emergency lane, in the parking lot beside ours, and isn't a trucker at all but a cowboy, holding his phone up I so I know who I'm talking to. His truck is beside him. It's a king cab dually with fairing and running lights and sponsors all over it. Attached to it is a trailer that looks like a deluxe camper for fifty.

"How many?" I ask him, because the windows of his truck are black.

He leans forward, trying to see me better through the window.

"How many you got?" he says back.

I lower my goggles into place, shrug into the padded shoulder claws of the tray.

Eight is how many, it looks like. Six Johns, two Janes, one over-flow and the coffee can for tip. And he should only have six seat-belts in that cab.

For all I know though, his whole trailer's packed shoulder-to-shoulder with rodeo clowns.

There's no reason today should be different than any other, I suppose.

I do the straps of the tray—they're what got my dad in trouble, when the trucker opened his door—add two more Janes just in case, then maneuver myself out the front door, walk across the drive-through the same way pregnant women walk at the mall: leaning back, one hand on my hip, my top lip curled.

"Good thinking," the cowboy says, about my goggles.

I don't say anything.

Close now, I can see it's just him in the truck. And that the camper's a horse trailer.

Painted on the side of it is *Roundabout Buttercup 3000*.

"Boy or girl?" I say.

"What?"

"Your horse."

"Oh, *Three*," the cowboy says, tipping his hat back. "I think three'll have it done."

"First time?"

He nods, lets it turn into a spit that takes probably five seconds.

"And all-American male," he says, patting the side of the trail-er. "Think I'd cut the golden goose?"

I just stare at him, waiting for him to make his selection.

"These are all, then?" he says, about the Johns.

"We have curtains, too," I say, jiggling the tray a bit so the cur-tains all around the edge dance a little.

The way my dad has them velcroed on, they look either like a large skirt for me or like they're supposed to be hiding whoever's about to stick their hands up through the holes, for the worst puppet show ever in the history of anything.

"For privacy," I add, my hand still to the curtain. "They're supposed to attach to your headliner."

He looks back to his truck, gets it.

"No curtains," he says, smiling, "but thanks."

I shrug like it's just a service, not an Upsale, and he takes one of the Johns, holds it up to inspect it. I try to focus only on the blue lettering on his chrome-edged mud flap. Not because it's interesting, but because when the customer's out of his vehicle, there are all kinds of new awkwardnesses.

If they get back in their vehicle to fill their John or Jane, then they're hiding. Or they think I want to look. But if they stand right there in front of me, so that if they didn't have the John my shins would be getting splattered, then we both know they're peeing on me, in a way.

The good part about that is that when you get any backsplash while somebody's watching, it counts, and you have no choice but to wash your hands then.

Maybe Collins is right, a little. We are bringing urinal etiquette out into the world.

"Half-dollar a pop?" the cowboy says, taking another John up from the tray.

"Forty-nine cents," I say back. "So that'll be four, then?"

"You don't know who he is, do you?" he says, smiling at me past the new John.

"Who?"

"You know in the Bible how it says that death came too, on a pale horse?"

He pats the trailer again, so that Roundabout Buttercup 3000 stamps back.

"This is that horse, man," he whispers, biting his lip at the end of it, his eyes hot. "We win Belmont next week, every other horse in the world might as well be dead."

"So he's fast?"

"Why you think we named him Buttercup?"

I nod like this means something, look at the trailer, and then a pair of headlights ease in from the road.

A red Firebird, taking the dip one tire at a time, like it's slinking back.

I turn back to the cowboy.

"Four, then," I hear myself say.

He spits again, says "Can we wait to tally until it's all said and done, maybe?" He makes for his wallet. "I can do a deposit if you need..."

I narrow my eyes at the cab of his truck again—still empty—then look at the trailer.

"I thought there was just Buttercup in here?" I say.

"That's his daddy's name. He's Three."

It's complicated, animal husbandy. Especially when I'm not really listening anymore.

Instead of pulling into the drive-through, Mark's Firebird is stopped just past the entrance, the headlights folded back down into the nose.

I look for my staring spot on the next building over but can't find it from this angle. It makes me feel like I'm falling.

"Ready?" the cowboy says, and, like with Buttercup, I realize again that we're talking two totally separate languages here.

"Whenever," I say, because it's policy not to rush the customer.

I don't want to have to go back to warm up the glove, I mean. And Mark and Prudence are still back there watching me, watching this. Waiting to apologize for the M60, probably, their serious faces on.

The lump in my throat is a water balloon, filling.

The reason people steal our curtains sometimes is because they can make the front seat of a car into a bedroom, if you stick them up by the window, say, instead of between the two seats. And the one Mark has, it even matches his seats.

What I want to do is scurry away, off into the darkness. Leave the tray by some other building, for my dad to find in the morning.

What I *don't* want is to stand here even one second longer.

I could be delivering urinal cake, right? That's almost like having a Coke route or something.

"You sure you're okay with this?" the cowboy says, his head turned sideways so he can look at me with just one eye.

"It's what I do," I say back to him, flicking my eyes to the Firebird one last time, on accident.

What I'm doing is breaking up with her in my head. So I can keep a normal face on when she does it for real, a minute from now.

"Okay then," he says, and steps around me, to the trailer gate. I follow not because I trust him or because of policy, but because I'm showing Prudence that she's made the right decision. That this is who she's been dating since the sixth grade. That I have amoebas on my hands, my face, all over me. In my mind. That my tears would be yellow, if I was going to cry over any of this.

But I'm not.

She should be with somebody else, somebody better.

Nobody should be with me.

That's just the way the world is. Like Collins said, I'm a pragmatist.

When the cowboy offers his hand to pull me up into the trailer behind him, I don't even look back to her to nod bye. Instead I just rise up, away from her, my eyes hotter than I want them to be.

The rest of me, though, it's ice cold.

I know what this is now.

My school bus fears have been childish.

Looking at us around his shoulder, his nostrils tasting the air, Roundabout Buttercup 3000.

"I know he can fill at least eight," the cowboy says, patting the horse on the rump, the horse's tail swishing to brush his hand. "Anymore than that, we'll have to...*improvise.* Oh, and you might want to step out of that peanut rig. Don't want to spook him." He smiles then, slaps Buttercup harder. "Not that he's shy, mind you."

The water balloon in my throat has burst, is drowning me.

The cowboy narrows his eyes at me, bites his lip again.

"I only need to save back a quart," he says. "The Commission'll pull blood after the race, of course, but we like to do a little in-house quality control ourselves. See if he's throwing protein or... well. Just see what all's still showing up. What isn't."

Roundabout Buttercup 3000 looks back, his eyes cue balls, and snorts my smell out.

"This *is* what y'all do, isn't it?" the cowboy says.

In the silence that follows, I swallow, gag a little, and finally nod, lower myself to my knees to duck out from under the tray.

"You mind closing that?" I ask, the gate, and for a few moments after he does, before the overhead lights glow on, the trailer is pitch black. Just Roundabout Buttercup 3000 breathing in, out, in, out.

"Think I saw a show like this down in Juarez once," the cowboy whispers, like church.

I stand, adjust my goggles, tighten my gloves, and ask him to please be quiet.

34.

The Firebird is still in the same place when I step down from the trailer, the tray sloshing with gallons of horse pee, almost pulling me back to my knees.

Maybe the next generation of trays will have gurney wheels on the front, that we can fold down. And a WIDE LOAD sign. And a mask, so nobody will know who we are. A built-in therapy headset. A Dicta-Will in case we just keep walking one day, out into traffic.

I stare at the dark windshield of the Firebird, waiting, and then the driver's door opens, the dome light glowing down on just Prudence.

I don't know if this is worse or better.

She follows me to the Hut, puts her hand to my wrist just as I'm pulling against the door.

I stop, just stare at my reflection in the glass.

"I didn't tell the police," I say. "If that's what you're worried about."

She lets her hand rasp away.

"Look at me," she says.

I don't.

"You should have," she says.

"What?"

"Told the police."

"Your mom would really like that."

"You should have been mad, I mean," she says.

I shrug like it didn't really matter.

"I tried to stop him," she says.

"I could tell, yeah. This is where I say thanks, right?"

She turns, her arms crossed, and walks over to the broken-down tables of Rocket Burger. They're white with uric acid. Because birds can read. They know what The Bladder Hut's for.

I stare up at the top of the door for long seconds then close my eyes, decide a hundred times just to go inside.

But I don't.

I kneel down to step out of the tray then bring over two curtains, set them like placemats over the sludgy seats of two different tables.

It's the cruelest thing I can think of.

She takes one and I straddle the other, start fraying out a corner where my mom's seam got confused.

Prudence is crying, yeah.

I steal one look at her, then two.

"He thinks I'm getting my phone from your car," she finally says, flashing her cell like that's proof of who she's lying to here.

I lift one shoulder in response.

It's good that she snuck away to talk to me, I suppose, but bad that he trusts her with his keys after just two hours. So it's nothing.

"It wasn't a *date*," she whispers. "I know that's what you're thinking."

"He get a good picture for the yearbook?" I say back.

She closes her eyes tighter.

"You don't have to be like this," she tells me.

"I know. I'm sorry. Congratulations are in order, right?"

She looks up to me, doesn't look away.

"It was Chickenstein," she says, her voice more level now, and pointed directly at me. "Chickenstein was at the mall, okay? *Everybody* was going there. I just happened to jump in his car."

What she's talking about is how, an hour or two before some games, Chickenstein gets dropped somewhere by the radio station van, starts scalping tickets. Except it's legal.

That explains why the news vans never showed, I suppose.

"And then it just turned into something else," I say for her. "I know. It's a sweet car. He's a football player. And he's really funny."

She's still staring at me.

"I'm trying to say I understand," I add, nothing defensive at all in my voice. "I wouldn't stay with me either." I shrug, stare down at the corner of my curtain.

"You could work here forever," she says, almost a whisper.

I flash my eyes up to her.

She doesn't blink.

For a moment I falter, can remember her in band when I first met her, her trombone heavier than she was, and her showing up Christmas morning our seventh grade year, so I could not even notice the new boots she was wearing, and the way I used to decorate her locker, and how she used to pretend not to like her chocolate milk just so I could have it, and a hundred other things, enough that my hand, without me even telling it to, reaches up to lift her chin the way I always do, to get her lips angled right.

But I've still got the gloves on.

Prudence shies away.

I laugh through my nose, nod, and suddenly my shadow splashes across her.

Headlights, pulling in.

"No, no—" she says, pulling at my wrist again, to show me, to push my hand against her face, but I'm already walking away.

"Got a customer," I'm saying, reciting off some teleprompter in my head. "We're not supposed to use company time for personal business. And we—we don't have any more personal business."

The track starts up, the whole Bladder Hut shuddering awake.

I stand into the tray, fall imediately in love with the way the weight presses down on me. It needs to be twice as much, really. I can carry anything.

"I'm sorry," I say to her, sitting on a curtain in the home of what was to be the world-famous Poo Burger.

The customer has to pull around again when I don't make it to the pedal in time.

It's a family.

The dad looks at a place beside me and asks if I'm all right, if there's anyone he can call, anything he can do?

"Why?" I say back, handing him his John and Jane, his Little John and Baby Jane.

I'm the best actor in the world.

At least until he leaves, and I see Mark Broyles' red Firebird making a forty-two point turn to get angled out the entrance, then pulling into the road without any headlights.

Four years gone is one way to look at it.

Another way is how her hand felt on my wrist, even through the glove. Will that be enough for the rest of my life? It'll have to be.

I go back to my place under the counter, close my eyes tight, finally sling my goggles down the hall.

They slide for about eight feet, then splash to a stop.

I open my eyes back up.

35.

I don't want him up here, but Tandy's still sitting shell-shocked on her bus, probably not getting off for three states, and Roy's surely in some holding facility at the Cockfight, not even showing up by eight-thirty in the morning, and Mom's at—she's not talking about books anyway, I'm pretty sure—so I climb up onto the counter, call my dad's cell, and close my eyes when he answers.

"What's the first thing you learn at Drive-Through U.?" he says into the phone, his breath strained like he's leaned down by the steering wheel, trying to make his car look empty. Probably while he's sitting at a red light, yeah.

I open my eyes, focus on the sheen of pee coating the tile floor.

Will insurance cover this?

Do we even have insurance?

On our wall where the fire extinguisher should be is a gift from one of my dad's church friends. It's a miniature wooden paddle behind glass. So that when business gets too good, we can row to safety. In our miniature boat.

"I know, I know," I say back to my dad. "Listen, I—"

"*What's the first thing,*" he says again. Behind him now, the whine of sirens.

"They're onto you," I say, calmer than I would have ever thought possible.

He sobs yes, then keeps saying it, then hangs up in a squeal of tires. The kind that come before a hail of bullets.

Next I call Mom but get dumped to her voicemail like I knew would happen: book club night trumps all.

"It's—it's Dad," I tell her, and then my voice cracks a little. "And—and it's not your fault I didn't wash my hands. I *know* to. Really. I wasn't even…I was just—I was just. Smoking, okay? And. It's Dad. I don't know. I think he, like, needs to talk or something."

There's no way to call other people's voicemail back and delete your message.

I settle the receiver back onto its cradle, hold it there to keep myself balanced, and look down the hall.

Chris Raines' meth-head door wasn't built for this kind of pressure, for this kind of night.

Neither was I.

And then a man in a preacher shirt is knocking on the glass.

I look over from my perch.

He smiles, nods that yes, he's real.

I look to all the floor between me and the window, then back to him, and lift the phone. He nods, steps back to read the phone number off our wall.

As for why the tracks haven't started, my best guess it that the pee's shorted out the floor pedal.

Meaning it could be septic *and* electric.

When the phone beside me rings I almost fall off the counter. I'm so naked without my goggles.

"Bladder Hut," I say, the customer service in my voice just automatic now.

"This is God," the preacher says. "I need you to build something for me."

I lower the phone to my shoulder, shrink into myself a little more.

Now the guy's laughing.

I can tell he's really a preacher because of that. The fake ones— and there's more than you'd think, like it's some kind of rush to put on a collar, try to molest the drive-through personnel—never make any jokes, because jokes are what sinners are always trying to pull.

I don't know.

With my luck, he's here for copyright infringement: the Bible had the name "John" first, and already had him associated with flowing water.

I'm going to hell. It's no secret.

It'll probably be a step up from here, anyway.

But then the preacher waggles his own packet of brochures up by his face.

"Suggestion box out back," I say, tilting my head to show.

"It's full," he says into his cell, his voice so tolerant, the smile in his eyes beaming, steady.

"And wet?" I ask.

It's always wet at night. We tried painting it different colors, but finally just gave up, left it porcelain white like tooth enamel. Drilled drain holes in the bottom.

"Just leave it on the—" I say, then lean far enough forward to be able to pull the window crank for him, to show.

The preacher sets the packet up on the window ledge, pats it twice in thanks, in blessing, to keep it there.

We each hang our phones up, and it's almost awkward.

"Would some scripture help, you think?" he says now that we can talk, his face that hesitant kind of jokey. "Something from Job, perhaps?"

I almost smile with him now, until I see that's exactly what he's wanting. This is what he does: make people feel better. Let the world be a tolerable place for a moment or two.

"Anything on Noah?" I say back, my voice just flat, and this time I don't even flinch when the phone beside me rumbles in my ear.

I sit down on the counter so my feet are hanging down over the rising pee.

"Anything else?" I say through the window, the phone on my shoulder now.

"Well," the preacher says, shrugging, that smile still in his eyes, "I guess since I'm here and all, I could probably manage some, um, final rites..."

I pull a John over, spiral it through the window.

"You'll have to pull forward yourself," I say. "Just leave it on the—just take it if you want."

"Take it?"

From my shoulder, the phone, somebody's screaming, I'm pretty sure.

Dad.

"Or leave it," I say, "whatever," and the preacher understands I need to catch my call, lifts his left hand bye, his right already at his zipper, his cell trembling on the dash, ramping up into some hymn.

I lower my head to the phone, already squinting.

My dad's not screaming anymore, is just driving hard, the phone still on so I can hear the sirens.

But then they get louder, and doubled, and the cell signal cuts out a bit.

They're coming here.

He's bringing the police *here*.

I step down into the tacky, fermented urine and slosh over to the window just in time to see my dad's grand-opening Camaro streak by in the turn lane, pulling cop cars behind him like tin cans.

A full thirty seconds after the preacher's gone, then, his John the Baptist—I guess that's we'll start calling clerical Johns now—balanced on the ledge of the second window, the tracks grind forward for a few feet, The Bladder Hut trying to shake off the night, it feels like.

It's nine o'clock.

36.

Just as the street a few blocks down starts flashing red with pursuit, the Yellow Line rings one more time. I pick it up without preparing myself, but all it is is the game—Bantams fans screaming, stomping, throwing stuff down onto the ice. Hating the Woodpeckers.

Prudence.

I can't even hear her voice above it all, and I can't even guess why she's calling anyway.

To let me know she made it back safe? To rub it in?

Or maybe the call button just got pressed on accident, and I'm about to hear something I don't want to.

"Bladder Hut," I say, and then hang up, suck my cheeks in just to try not to think.

It could be that she saw Roy, I suppose.

Or wanted to say some perfect thing.

But it doesn't matter. Whatever she had to say, I wouldn't have been able to hear it, probably wouldn't have tried.

Really, I would have memorized each letter, each breath that made up each sound, each word, and then punished myself with that for months. Lived on it.

Though the pee is only about four inches up the wall—not even to the top of the industrial baseboard—I can see the line of dark wetness goes nearly up to the handle of Chris Raines' door.

The bay is lost.

Because of me.

Like my dad said, lecturing me about hygiene: I could bring this whole place down.

It didn't sound so bad then.

But not like this. I didn't want it like this.

Maybe it'll be one less thing to get split in divorce court, anyway.

Two years to go. Two years until I'm gone, until I blast off, start over, forget all this.

And then I see the red lights flashing on the buildings up the street, already know I'm going to remember them forever.

Dad.

He's trying to outrun the cops, but it's more than that, too. I think when you get to be his age, you've probably done enough stupid stuff that it all just keeps piling up behind you, then finally starts to fall over one day, and all you can do then is try to keep ahead of it. Not get crushed.

It's like a cartoon. This guy who's supposed to be raising me, I mean.

About four seconds after the sirens start painting the buildings red, I hear them, lean a little farther out the window.

Why he's circling the Hut instead of leading the cops out of town, I have no idea. He's never done this before, I guess, doesn't really have a plan. Has always seen himself at the front of a parade instead of leading a train of black-and-whites. A maverick, not an outlaw.

The night air is cool on my face, humid behind me.

I tap my foot, waiting for my dad to slam past again, but the toe of my shoe splashes pee up onto my other pants leg.

I look down to see it and then my dad's not slamming past at all, but sliding in, the back of the Camaro trying to get ahead of him, the tires boiling smoke.

"Dad," I say, gripping the counter tighter than I mean to.

The cops, with their obstacle course training, swing a bit wider to make The Bladder Hut entrance, but this gets them onto the slick leftover from the crashed-over port-a-potty, and they go sailing by, all sound and light and locked-up brakes.

The last I see before the intersection swallows them is Officer Spinrad, holding his coffee cup with his mouth, both hands climbing the wheel, trying to turn him into the slide.

I'm proud of my dad, yeah.

He clamps the Camaro to a sudden stop right in front of me, reaches up, his hand shaped like a—like a—

Like a John.

"Not supposed to serve family in the drive-through," I recite, holding the John back.

He's breathing hard, can't even talk, just leans up far enough for one of the backup Johns just inside the window.

"Like a curtain, sir?" I say after he's pulled forward, into the space between windows. "Glove?"

Because he has his own keys, he makes it the fourteen feet in something like twenty-two seconds, sets his bottle up on the ledge by the preacher's then leans back into his seat and closes his eyes, laughs to himself for a chuckle or two.

I angle my head out the window, can see lined up behind him, along the fifty-two second stretch, a string of beer bottles. Some his, some not.

I look back to him about this and he nods, filling his eyes with everything he wants me to know, and then Spinrad, out of breath himself from chugging all the way in from the intersection, is dragging my dad up through his window, pushing him against the stucco wall.

"That's ours," he informs me, pointing a gloved finger to my dad's John. The beer inside is still swirling, even has some head.

I put my hands over it, pull it back across the window track.

And now my dad's looking at me again, his eyes on fire.

I nod, get it, have been through Drive-Through U., yes. About twenty times.

"We don't redistribute, Officer," I say, talking slow and deliberate. "That's part of our customer service pledge. The most important part, even. Number *one*, you could say."

Spinrad looks to me, to my dad, then slings my dad back across the Camaro's hatch so he can reach in for the evidence my dad's John won't be.

Because the floor's slick, too, I can't move fast enough.

He gets a gloved hand around the John, puts his weight behind it.

I set my right foot against the wall on my side, shake my head no, and pull back with everything I have, both arms, say it again, the first thing I learned, the number one rule: "This. Is. *Ours!*"

He's twice as heavy as me, though, and already amped from the chase.

But then my dad jumps on him from behind, and we're a team suddenly, and I'm falling back, the John in my hands like a football, and I hold onto it no matter what I splash into, roll to cover it, then rise with it cradled against my chest, my teeth set, my eyes just as hot as my dad's.

Spinrad is staring at me through the window, his chest rising and falling.

"Kid," he says. "You don't even know what you're starting here."

I stare at him, then flash my eyes down to the preacher's John, still there on the ledge, rocking back and forth.

Spinrad sees me see it, and smiles. Takes it in his hand.

"It's fake," I say, stepping forward. "I don't know, you tell me— what do you call it, DUI...*N*? Driving under the influence of *nothing*? You can really get a ticket for imitation beer? What's the legal limit for that in Texas this year?"

"Give me a break. He's driving like a—"

"Like he's sad? Like he's been reaching into toilets for his whole life, looking for gold, for love, for something to hold onto?"

Hopefully my dad's unconscious, knocked out on the tracks.

But I kind of doubt it.

And I kind of don't want him to be, either.

Spinrad looks at me for a long time, gauging, then says, "If it's fake, let me have it then."

"We don't redistribute."

"But it's not piss. I know the trick, kid."

"I can't."

"The whole rest of your life is worth this?" he says, his voice almost a growl now.

"Twice over," I whisper to him, no customer service at all.

Spinrad doesn't even look down, just licks his lips, cocks his head to the side and thumbs his shoulder rig open.

He stops when he sees what I'm doing, though: unscrewing the top of my dad's John. Breathing hard, my lips either twitching or trembling, I can't tell, but I can't stop them either way.

"Watch," I tell him, then close my eyes, lick my lips, and lift the John to my mouth, letting it wash down my throat, over my chest, onto the floor.

When it's all gone I wipe my mouth with the back of my arm, sling the drops away.

"That proves it's not piss," Spinrad says. "Not that it's fake beer."

"And if it isn't?"

"Then I haul you both in. You for Minor in Possession and for smarting off to a peace officer, him for DUI, maybe even Public Intoxication. Resisting Arrest. Being a *freak*."

"That's what you want, isn't it?" I say to him. "Throw us both in jail? In the drunk tank?"

"In the *stupid* tank. The *toilet* tank."

"Then do it," I tell him, nodding to the John he's holding. "Michelob or Budweiser, Officer?"

"Coors," my dad says, his voice not faltering even a little, and Officer Spinrad wheels his eyes over to him, snarls his top lip up.

"The Coors was already gone," I say to my dad, staring right into Officer Spinrad's soul.

"I bought more," my dad says.

When Spinrad looks over to me about this I shrug, calling him on it—it's a move I've seen ten thousand times in all the locker rooms of my life—and Spinrad bares his teeth, unscrews the top of his John, and raises it to his mouth, gets a big, warm mouthful.

Worth it twice over, I say again, in my head, my pupils slamming shut and open as fast as they can, like a camera shutter.

For a moment more intimate than any I've ever had, Spinrad looks at me down along the John, and then his thick upper body is curling around itself, trying to heave this memory up before it can set.

He never gets the chance.

Just then, the pedal at the first window unshorts for another jerk, the tracks lurching forward two or three feet, enough to tip the rest of the preacher's holy water into Spinrad's face, and all down his polyester.

I drop my empty John down into the slurry on my side, and between my fingers and the floor, there's a lifetime.

37.

The videogame version of The Bladder Hut would be a first-person shooter. I know because I sit in the window for twenty minutes, arcing an imaginary line of pee at all the cops that pull into our parking lot to bite their lips, try not to laugh in an obvious way at Spinrad.

Two of them he throws bottles at.

One of them calls in a crime scene photographer.

A news van comes instead, the cameraman lumbering up through the slid-open door, his eyes settling immediately on my dad, still cuffed, bleeding around his right eye, not fighting anymore.

The good thing about running a business they don't even have zoning laws for, I guess, is that you're always first in line for public sympathy.

The smiling cops step into a casual wall in front of my dad—policy, I'm sure—one of them snapping my dad's cuffs open, ushering him away the way I've seen Saturday afternoon fathers try to herd baby birds out of the path of lawnmowers. It's not that they care about the birds, just that they don't want to make a mess.

My dad pulls his car out of the drive-through, parks it along-side mine then just sits there until I have to look away.

He's staring at his windshield. Seeing his whole life there may-be, swirling down the toilet.

I look around at the toilet I'm standing in.

The pee's up to my laces now, is soaking into my socks. The drive-through jerks forward every time a spark crosses in the pedal.

I put on the gloves we're supposed to wear to pull a milk tray off the bread rack—the gloves are electrician grade, in case the top of the rack ever crunches into one of the fluorescent lights—set the tray up on top of our soggy phonebook, work it up and down a few times then step up onto dry land. Dry-*ish* land. And then, nudge by nudge, I raise the cord that raised the pedal, hold it up higher and and higher. If I had my goggles on, I might blow into it, but already my knees are wet from kneeling down, and I've had my one wipie bath of the day.

I stand all the way and watch the pedal for a few seconds, to see if it's still going to be shorting or not, and, on cue, the tracks shudder.

I swing the pedal gently on the wall under the counter, delicate yellow beads floating in my breathing air, then place it on the se-cret shelf Roy keeps his coffee on.

Now the tracks are just grinding and grinding.

I push the pedal down to stop them, just an automatic response, and understand at last: they're doing what they're supposed to do.

We've got a customer.

I come up to the window, the heavy gloves still on, my pants a lost cause, my hair jagged through my hairnet.

"Sorry, we're—" I start.

It's Prudence.

She's still in Mark's Firebird, has it in slow reverse just to stay in one place. It's the single sexiest act I've ever seen.

She catches my eyes with hers for a moment then looks back to the dashboard.

"John or Jane," I ask.

She holds her hand out, says, simply, quietly, "You know I

still don't hate you, right? That I'll always never hate you? That I wouldn't even know *how?*"

I hand her a Jane, our fingertips whispering against each other, then step off the pedal, let her slip away.

For the next fifty-two seconds I slosh forward, trying to pace her, and know that this is how it starts. That there *is* a messed-up chromosome in my family, that there's nothing at all special about her peeing right beside me, except for the wall. That it's stupid, even, to attach all that to something everybody has to do anyway. That it doesn't mean anything.

Except she's never been through before, and is under strict orders from her mother never to, no matter what, and she doesn't want to anyway.

She hands me her warm Jane—it's a Shame Jane, an Apology Jane, an Uncalamity Jane—and fifty cents, and, because we're still broken up, I give her back the extra penny.

"You're supposed to take the keys," she reminds me.

"I don't want his keys," I say back.

She's about to cry again.

Her pee is warm even through the glove.

"Why'd you call?" I ask.

She studies Mark's dash all over, looks up to me like a question.

"A few minutes ago," I tell her.

In answer she passes her cell up. I know her security code, flip immediately to calls made.

The Bladder Hut's not there.

I give the phone back.

"No personal business," she says then, quoting me, her lips too firm. "Just customers, right?"

"You don't have to—" I start, but she's already pulling away again.

The thing about first-person shooter games is that you can't ever shoot yourself.

Maybe there's a reason for that.

I rack her Jane with all the rest then keep my hand there on it.

It's the closest I've come, this warmth. The exact temperature of love.

I've got the bottle back in my hands again, am thinking hard about twisting the lid off when my dad steps through the back door.

"I like that car," he says, splashing down into the second window area. Just studying his shoes instead of saying anything.

"It's a Firebird," I say.

He nods, looks out across the parking lot at his Camaro, as if comparing, and liking what he sees—he would—then makes his way down to the hall, not even lifting his feet.

I follow.

Where he's going is the PISO MOJADO unisex bathroom.

He doesn't shut the door either.

"Dad?" I say, Prudence's Jane still warm against my chest.

He doesn't answer, just straddles the toilet, lifts the lid off the tank and balances it on the sink.

From the water he pulls up an emergency fake beer.

Before he peels the cap off, he reaches in again, his sleeve going dark, and comes up with a plastic baggie of cigarettes. Tandy's brand.

He tosses them to me, the water misting my face.

"Don't tell your mother," he says, and then sits on the toilet and drinks like each mouthful is going to be his last. I stand in the hall and smoke one cigarette down to the butt, then another, until I get the nerve to say, about what's probably his fiftieth fake beer of the day, "Speaking of Mom—"

The reason I don't finish is that just then the lower hinge of Chris Raines' door to the bay gives, and a yellow, hip-level wall of urine is crashing down the hall towards me.

It looks less like the end of the world, more like a sun-faded painting over a motel bed when you're on vacation and every place not your own is magic, sort of.

Because there's still a drag or two left on it, I hold Tandy's cigarette up, to keep it dry.

And then I close my eyes.

38.

The next few moments are what heaven's like, I think: floating in a sea of golden, swirling light, your skin neither cold nor hot, just perfect, your lips calmly pressed together, as if you've been expecting this your whole life. And then there's a strong hand grazing just your fingertips like a promise, then circling your wrist, the other arm finding your waist.

I'm taller than my dad, but he still stands with me cradled to his chest, pulls me up past the surface, the pee streaming off his face, his eyes open in it.

Behind him and to the left, where the customers at the first window can't see it, is the one piece of workplace humor that ever met with his approval. It's the last dry thing in the place, I think, just a single-panel comic strip—a two story outhouse, with stairs going up to the second floor, a guy standing a few feet away, unsure whether he wants to pay five dollars for the upstairs door or ten cents for the lower one.

It's page one of that yellow bible in my dad's head, and all Drive-Through U. graduates have laminated versions to carry in their wallets, with an explanation on back, about the half-moon symbol on the outhouse doors, how it's some Norman Rockwell thing for just half your ass showing while you pee, instead of the whole thing, which would be a full moon.

He doesn't know when to stop, no. He doesn't even know that he maybe should.

But I'm not sure any other dad would have dove into the flood for me either, then held me like he is now.

When the urine's down to just our knees again, he lowers me back to where I can stand on my own.

"Well, shit," he says.

"Not exactly," I say, and catch his eye, and he smiles.

"That was a good catch earlier," he says, spinning a stray John at me like a football.

I don't fumble it, just pull it in.

And then I think of Collins. Of that bagged urinal cake.

It can wait.

Bobbing down the hall, moving with the current, is Prudence's Jane.

Past it, at the first window, the soft beige top of a red Firebird. I wade down.

Prudence looks up at me, her eyebrows coming together for a moment in worry but we're still broken up. She looks away instead, tenses her lips, and I lean down onto my elbows. To say what, I don't know—there's no perfect thing—but then I don't have to say anything.

Both Mark's cup holders are full. Not with old drinks, but with new ones, so cold drops are still beading on the plastic lids. Purpleliscious Rex.

And on the passenger seat, in four cardboard trays that they'll only give you if you ask, sixteen more frozen purple drinks.

Prudence stares straight ahead and cracks a roll of quarters open on the top of the steering wheel, her hand cupped around them so they won't spill.

"I've got all night," she says, having to blink something away, then finally wipes it with the cuff of the jacket she's wearing.

It's the same thing she kept doing that morning she walked over to my house on Christmas morning, her family waiting at her house for her, blocks away.

I hadn't known what to do then, either.

There was no handbook, I mean. No policy.

If Collins were here, he'd have the answer for me: there never is a handbook. There's just trying. And holding on.

"Who is it?" my dad calls from the bathroom, and I look down the hall, just stalling, and then come back to her, her eyes so open.

"P," I say down to her, "it's P," and she looks up to me, the corners of her mouth ghosting up into a smile.

"You're all wet," she says.

"Initiation," I tell her, flicking my eyes away.

She plays along: "So you're in now?"

"The toilet, yeah."

"Room for two?" she asks.

"Always," I tell her, my chin tensed into a prune.

"So we still on for the game?" she says.

I reach into my back pocket for the tickets but they're matted in with the old man's brochure. All I can do is set them on the counter.

Prudence pulls two stubs from Mark's visor.

"Chickenstein?" I say.

"They were in an egg," she says, starting to laugh a little.

It's the way Chickenstein sells them.

I live in the stupidest city in the world, I'm pretty sure.

Maybe forever.

39.

Before I can slip out, Roy's extra clothes balled under my arm, four looted quarters for the truck stop shower down the road—like Prudence doesn't have a roll—a curious thing happens: my left pants pocket starts smoking.

My dad's in the bathroom flushing the toilet over and over, trying to bail out The Bladder Hut one and a half gallons at a time, his siphon hose started in the worst way ever, so he doesn't see me snake them, and Prudence is parked out at the curb, Mark's passenger seat lined with all the lap protectors and curtains I had by the window, so I'm alone.

What I think, the smoke trailing up my side, along my jawline, is that I can't blow up now. Not tonight. Not when I've got my whole life planned. Not when it's all finally going perfect.

Already I can tell Prudence is going to marry me, I mean, and that we're going to be together for always and that there are never going to be any more Gatorade bottles in the top of my locker.

It's all pretend, though.

I'm one of those people born with a kill switch: if too many happy endorphins ever start coursing through my system, my self-destruct activates, starts ticking down.

I move my lips to try to call my dad but nothing comes out.

The Cockfight is years away already. A joke. Roy's backup clothes fall away, in slow motion, like the person in them just evaporated.

Maybe this is what you get for too many underage cigarettes: after your ten thousandth, you spring a leak, and then your tongue turns to ash, your blood to tar, and all the capillaries in your brain constrict until you can't think at all.

And I still can't make a sound.

Shaking my head no the whole way, I balance along the wall, down to the bathroom. My dad's standing in front of the toilet, the index and middle fingers of his left hand to the chrome flush handle.

"Piso mojado," he says without looking up, "right?"

"Dad," I creak.

He flushes again, tracks the water around and around like a child, and then the bowl fills again, from the outside.

"*Dad*," I say again, and he looks up, his lips loose, unprepared.

My eyes are wet, I know. A different wet than the rest of me.

"Well, uh-oh," my dad says about the smoke rising from my pants, and, just so I'll have a witness, I reach into the guilty pocket, into the fog, the steam, and come up with the only thing there: the bagged urinal cake the health inspector gave me.

I didn't reseal it, so the pee seeped inside.

I switch hands to hold the bag more by the corner and the cake rolls out, plunks into the pee, starts fizzing like an Alka-Seltzer.

My dad can't really talk, is just shaking his head no. Like if a monster you'd been dreaming about was standing by your bed when you woke.

"Where did you get that?" he says.

"No, Dad, it's all right—" I start, about to smile because this is so stupid, but he's already wrapped around me, pulling me away from the steam fizzing up from the spinning cake.

"No!" he screams, in a way that makes me crank my head over, study him, and then he's saving me again, dragging and pushing me ahead of him, out the front of The Bladder Hut, the pee spilling out the door behind us.

We don't stop there, either, but keep running and stumbling almost all the way to the road.

Standing there waiting for us, his face smooth with wonder, is Roy.

He's in full wetsuit gear again, my old snorkeling goggles chocked up on his forehead, a cigarette clamped between his teeth, his lips bloody around it, his left eye going blue.

Tucked under his left arm is an empty, unsigned Jane.

He lifts the wide black toe of his right foot so the quarter-inch high wall of urine can sigh past like the tide.

It doesn't even make it to the ball of his foot.

"Didn't kick that plug back in, did you?" he says to me, his lips hardly moving.

I don't think my dad hears this. Just to be safe, I don't answer.

The steam is fogging the windows now, coming out at the many seams of The Bladder Hut.

"Thought you threw all those bad boys the hell away," Roy says to my dad, pointing at the mess with his cigarette.

My dad is just staring. Breathing deep.

I start to ask *What bad boys?* but just hearing Roy say it like that, half in code, it's enough. I see it all in a rush, what I've probably known all along, just not admitted: my dad, pouring urinal cake batter from beaker to beaker in the garage—his dark years—then finally stumbling onto a dangerous mix. One that doesn't improve hygiene, but makes it worse.

It was with him at that Bantams game.

I look over to him about this but he's checked out. His fingers are moving along the seam of his slacks like he's about to run, and just keep running.

"I promised never again," he finally says, to Roy, I think, but just out loud, too. "It was…nobody was supposed to get hurt."

Roy laughs smoke, takes another drag, and says, tilting his head to the Hut, "Another accident like that, you can start a chain, kimo."

Finally my dad does look over to me, to see if I'm catching any of this.

I try to keep my face slack, innocent, but he sees anyway. Closes his eyes and keeps them closed.

It's what he does sometimes on the way to the refrigerator, for another fake beer. Like he's practicing to be blind. Pretending. Punishing himself. Beer after beer.

If he had a fake liver, it would be corroded from guilt.

Instead, he's just pushed my mom—wherever. Away. From the killer he's become. From the killer he now knows somebody else knows him as. From the killer *I* have to now know him as.

I close my eyes, too, to not have to think about it.

"Nobody was supposed to get hurt," he's still saying, like there's a magic number of times you can say it when it'll just become true.

"I meant to kick that plug in," I say, answering Roy at last, then I nod to The Bladder Hut, wait till Roy's cued in. "Can you…?" I say.

He smiles, takes another drag—he's on the butt now, I'm pretty sure—and holds his left hand up, fingers spread.

It's Roy-speak for *five minutes*. For *no problem*. For *child's play, kiddo*.

But there's a gleam in his eye I don't like.

"Tell your old man to call his *buddies*," he says, spitting the word. "They've got the trucks, the licenses."

"They only come on Saturdays," my dad says, like he's talking in his sleep.

And anyway, I know, there's too many people here. His Saturday friends are into private disposal, not media events.

I look to Roy again.

He smiles with half his mouth.

"Save it just out of the kindness of my heart?" he says, more to my dad than to me.

I get it a little bit, I think.

He worked on my dad's project in grad school or wherever, and the way my dad's paid him back is with the graveyard shift.

"What do you want?" my dad asks.

Roy holds up Cybil Leon's Jane, shakes it like it's obvious what he wants: celebrity urine to auction online.

I reach up, guide his Jane back down like it's yesterday's news.

My dad and him are both watching me now. Waiting.

"She came back?" Roy says, his voice hushed, eager.

"Somebody else?" my dad whispers, his hand to the back of my arm, so I won't leave before answering him.

I don't pull away, but lean in closer, look from one of them to the other.

"There's—there's a tray in there," I say. "The lids are all on tight. It hasn't been processed yet. Do you know of a horse called... called Buttercup, I think?"

Roy pans over to me slow, his neck flushing.

"Three *K*? Ran one-fifty-one in Baltimore, in the *rain*?"

I shrug sure, yeah. That one.

Roy lets the cigarette fall from his fingers, hiss into the thin coat of pee on the asphalt.

"You pulling my chain?" he says.

"Pale yellow horse," I say. "And Death came with him."

Roy's breathing deep now, almost smiling.

He looks to my dad and my dad nods once, looks away, and Roy settles the mask down over his eyes, extends his hand for me to shake it.

I do, my skin to his glove, and then he offers his hand to my dad.

My dad looks down to it, up to Roy, and over to the Hut.

"Captain's supposed to go down with his ship," he says, taking Roy's hand.

"Some other night, maybe," Roy says. "Some other boat. But not this one. Not if I have anything say about it."

My dad puts his other hand around the back of Roy's, nods, and then Roy's trudging across the parking lot, pushing through the glass door with the Tycho Brahe seal and walking into the fog, the door sealing shut behind him, like The Bladder Hut's just swallowed him whole.

"I know we don't redistribute," I say after a couple of minutes.

It's an apology.

My dad's upper body jerks in a kind of sick laugh.

"Not that sure we process livestock either," he says.

The muscles of my face are trying to smile.

"She waiting for you?" he says then.

Prudence, back by Mark's Firebird.

I nod.

"You should go," my dad says, watching her but seeing someone else. "It's not every girl who'll put up with...you know."

"It was the health inspector who gave me that," I say, finally.

My dad isn't surprised.

"He said something about a city contract," I add, a new thing rising in my voice.

My dad looks over to me for more.

"Eleven thousand urinals in the city," I recite.

"And he had to pick this one," my dad finishes.

I see Roy's hand reach out of the steam to plant itself on the glass window in front, like he's fighting some pee monster in there. Some hose with impossible pressure.

"Maybe that's the ticket," my dad says, his hands on his pockets. "The safe thing, right? This"—the Hut—"maybe it's just stupid."

It's the first time I've ever heard this in his voice.

It makes me cold, all the way to the middle. And scared. Ashamed.

"It is," I tell him. "It's worse than stupid. It's an insult to public decency. An affront to hygiene. The end of the human species as we know it."

My dad looks over to me, not sure where I'm going.

Him and me both, I guess.

"Doesn't mean I'm going to quit or anything, though," I hear myself say.

My dad breathes out, maybe for the first time since he pulled me from the flood, but then he squints in something like pain.

"But he's got me. Alfred P. Kayler."

It's the old man's name. The old man my dad *didn't* kill. The reason for fifty thousand fake beers.

I look over, start to tell him about the brochure, but then— I'm his son after all, and he's a businessman first—I negotiate a bit: "What would you say to moving Drive-Through U. to once a month, say, instead of every Saturday?"

He rubs a spot on his forehead, doesn't like this idea at all.

"You think that'll be enough?" he asks, almost a whisper, real concern in his eyes.

I raise one shoulder that it might be enough, yeah, and then have to cover my mouth with my hand.

It smells like pee.

Nothing new.

40.

Because Roy's got stuff pushed up against the front door now, we go in through the back, my dad collecting the comments from the suggestion box like always, and holding them out so they don't drip on him.

As I duck into the door I hold my finger up to Prudence—just one more minute.

After salvaging the retracted obituary, I'm going to try to peel the Cockfight tickets up from the brochure, because they're magic. Secret. Mine.

My dad balances the comments by the first window then splashes through to the bay—there's some sort of pump going, but at least the steam's gone—and I go straight to the lockers, to steal whatever other clothes I can.

Like I should have expected, Tandy's tucked into Roy's locker.

She pulls on the cigarette she's been filtering her air with, the cherry glowing down to a deep red, then passes the cigarette across to me, all her fingers extended, very ladylike.

"All *year*," she says.

It's how long I'm going to be spraying down the walls, for calling her up here tonight. For this single cigarette.

"Two," I say back to her, opening my hand for the rest of the pack.

She studies me to see if I'm joking, and, when I'm not, lobs the pack over.

"Starting tomorrow," she calls after me, through the locker she's still hiding in, her own sensory-deprivation tank, and I shift Roy's second ball of clothes to my other arm, high-step to the counter of the first window.

The brochure's still there—the urine never lapped that high, anyway—and the tickets, because they're made from slick cardboard, peel up easier than I thought.

Under them is the delicate black-and-white face of Alfred P. Kayler.

The paper's wet enough that I can just stick it to the glass, for my dad.

Outside now, Prudence is standing by the red Firebird, leaning over to see what's taking me so long.

I nod to myself, check my pockets for some reason, then realize I'm just stalling. That I don't really want to leave as bad I always have. That I'm going to miss this place someday.

I shake my head at how stupid I've become, tap Alfred P. Kayler's face with the tips of my fingers, and am already ducking away when a customer clatters up to the window, the tracks hollow under the car's tires.

I lean back to tell whoever it is about the truck stop down the road but then it's not even a person at all.

Behind the wheel, bigger than life and twice the dancer: Chickenstein.

For long moments he or she looks at me through his or her neck webbing, the costume head's large eyes staring at me too, pinning me in place, knowing everything.

It's a girl, a woman, I know.

Just from the tilt of the head.

It's the way mothers watch their kids when their kids don't know they're being watched.

But still, I say it like every time: "Both?"

Chickenstein nods, suddenly remembering why she's here— for a John *and* a Jane—then digs through the rental car's empty ashtrays and glove compartments and seats and finally into her own belly feathers.

All she comes up with is two quarters, dirty silver in her white glove.

I look back to the idea of my dad, to the idea of anybody, then work two of my shower quarters up from my wet pocket, flash them to Chickenstein.

She stares at me again, nods once, in eternal gratitude.

I pass the John through, then the Jane, and give her her privacy, go to the bay to tell my dad I'm out of here.

He waves without looking up, is trying to muscle some fitting over Old Faithful's drain plug, to pump everything back.

Roy, he's anywhere.

Inside the tank, probably, pulling on the fitting. Free-diving with Dick, no tank at all.

I don't want to help them, either.

Fifty cents doesn't make you a good person, I mean. Not even close.

I back away like I'm sneaking off, and push through the back door, the night air crisp enough now that the urine's steaming off me a little.

Because my sleeves are still wet, I sling as many drops onto the wall as I can, as high as I can, covering my old graffiti.

If I had the aim, or needed to pee, I'd tell Collins to take a long walk off a short dock. As it is, I just rub my cigarette out with the toe of my shoe then take a couple of steps forward, to slap the lid down on the suggestion box.

There's something in it, though. After my dad just emptied it.

I look over to Prudence but it's not from her. She'd be watching closer if it was. And she doesn't have the key for what this is anyway.

For about five seconds, I forget how to breathe.

It's the videotape of me not washing my hands. The only thing that could get me unindentured from my dad.

I look down along the side of the building, the way Chickenstein must have just gone, and smile with my mouth open.

Mom.

Every Tuesday night.

And then I'm laughing, about to fall down from it, until Prudence comes up, takes me by the arm, starts leading me to Mark's Firebird.

"My mom," I say to her, stringing the videotape out behind us. Feeding it to the night.

"You're still asking about her?" she says, starting to laugh with me, *at* me, even, and I shake my head no, yes, and finally just no.

Halfway to the Firebird, I look back to The Bladder Hut one last time.

Roy's at the second window now, sitting sideways on the stool so he can stick his arms out. What he's holding is the emergency paddle. What he's doing is rowing, leaning out as if to look ahead, make sure he's not about to hit anything.

"What's wrong with him?" Prudence whispers.

"Nothing," I tell her, and then there's my dad, in the first window. He's going through all my fake suggestions, then stopping, reading one in particular. Over and over.

What I wrote on the last one, in my mom's hand, was *Hey, Pottymouth. Call me.*

It's what I heard her call him once years ago, before I knew anything.

"Wait," I say to Prudence, holding my breath, walking backwards, and then my dad does it, actually breaks policy for her: he reaches back for the Yellow Line.

"No personal calls," I say to him quietly, nodding. "Business only."

"Come on," Prudence is saying beside me.

My dad even puts up his own sign: BATHROOM BREAK—BACK IN FIVE.

"He's got one *too*?" I say, and now Prudence turns me around, both her hands in both of mine, and she's already talking about the next big thing: "...like—like you like get a *Kleenex* at the first window, then the attendant at the second window holds a little trash can out for you to drop it in, right?"

Between windows, you blow your nose.

In the privacy of your own car.

"What kind of delay?" I ask.

"Twenty seconds?"

It sounds about right.

Blow 'n Go.

Pick and Roll.

I take her hand in mine.

"Think we can still catch the second period?"

"If you'd stop looking at me like that, yeah."

Like kids then, we pull each other the rest of the way across the parking lot, and when Prudence leans over the passenger door to kiss me on the lips, her breath is cherry and gritty, exactly like baby aspirin.

Acknowledgments

Will Christopher Baer said to me once that I really had that teen-angst thing *down*, man. I left thinking, cool, yeah, I do, I got it down, rock and roll. Except then I got to wondering if that had actually been a compliment or not. And I'm still wondering. All the same, stories about guys working all the windows you work, growing up—I walked roofs, I cleaned toilets, I hoed weeds and counted seeds, I drove tractor and moved pipe, I scraped water pumps for nine-hour shifts, I hung ceiling tile and taped and bedded and scraped and painted, and delivered firewood between, and dug more ditches and stretched more fences than I'll ever remember, and painted road stripes that went in anything but a straight line, and pushed enough carts to get us all to the moon and back twice—those stories about working are always so real to me. There's always somebody real *in* there, I mean. For *Flushboy*, that real person was my little brother, Skylar, some seventeen years younger than me. The voice, though, that vital bit I needed to make the story real, that's from a ride Judy Wilson gave me from Marshall, Minnesota to wherever the biggest airport close to there is. Her son made the drive with us, and, he was, I don't know, fourteen? Sixteen? And he didn't say much, but he said it right, such that, when I got back to Texas, I wrote *Flushboy* fast, before I lost the way he talked. The way *Flushboy* talks. And he's probably in college now, doesn't even remember taking a writer to the airport way back when. And, thanks to my agent Kate Garrick, for mailing out a drive-through urinal novel—her first, I'm thinking—and thanks to Dzanc and Dan Wickett and Steven Gillis, for being part of the revolution, and thanks to Matt Bell, for talking me out of at least a few of the "yeahs" I'm so prone to, and big Julia Roberts thanks to Guy Intoci, the editor who always makes me sound better and more sensible than I actually am—without him, this book isn't this book. Here's to many more with him. Also thanks to the stuff I'm stealing from this time: Tony Earley's "The Prophet From Jupiter"; Billy Joel's "Scenes from an Italian Restaurant"; Christopher Nolan's poem "Terminus"; *Seinfeld*'s "The Nap" episode; Adam Johnson's "Trauma Plate"; Christopher Moore's beta males. And, I would gladly have stolen from Stuart O'Nan's *Last Night at the Lobster* and Will Ferrell's hadrosaur urine theory in *Land of the Lost*, had I known them before writing this. Thanks to all those texts, and more besides. And thanks to my brothers Sean and Skylar, for believing in this novel way back in 2007, and insisting I mail it out, and passing it around to everybody they knew, and then getting me to print more copies. And thanks first and last to my wife Nancy, for understanding I needed to get this one down fast, before it slipped away. My computer was in the bedroom back then, remember? I tried to type quiet, but I always try, I know. And you always let me fail. Thank you thank you thank you.

9 781938 604171